~Half a Day Late~
The Battle of Crampton's Gap On South Mountain

Sean Daniels

Sean Daniels

for my mother, Evelyn

ISBN-13: 978-1986469494
ISBN-10: 1986469492

Brownsville area map and photo of Shafer Farm by Nathan Strong

Illustrations by Susan Carney
www.susancarney.com

Author's photo by Louis Covey

FOREWARD

Often historians and authors overlook the significance of the Battle of Crampton's Gap, considered the lesser of the three separate battles fought along South Mountain on September 14, 1862. Major-General George B. McClellan's overpowering force from the Army of the Potomac were trying to punch their way through Confederate forces at Turner and Fox's Gaps, considered the most heavily defended gaps along South Mountain. While General McClellan was waging the fight at Turner's and Fox's Gaps, Major-General William B. Franklin and his VI Corps were given the assignment of pushing through the Confederate force at Crampton's Gap. General Franklin's 12,800-man VI Corps gave him an overwhelming numeral superiority of 6 to 1 against the small Confederate force of 2,100 men under the command of Brigadier-General Howell Cobb.

The small Confederate force at Crampton's Gap and Brownsville Pass was basically acting as a rear guard to protect the other Confederate brigades, about 6,000 men belonging to Major-Generals Lafayette McLaws and Richard Anderson's divisions. They were being used to seal off Harpers Ferry and to capture Maryland Heights in conjunction with the rest of Major-General Thomas (Stonewall) Jackson's Confederate force, which was operating south of the Potomac River.

Harpers Ferry was very important to General Lee's plan while operating in Maryland. The reason is because Lee did not like the idea that 14,000 Union soldiers had the ability to operate on his line of communications and possibly hinder his operations in Maryland.

On September 14, while General George B. McClellan and the majority of his Army of the Potomac battled against Confederate forces defending Turner and Fox's Gaps on South Mountain near Boonsboro, 12 miles to the south near the Potomac River, Major-General William Franklin and his VI Corps were easily pushing their way through Crampton's Gap into Pleasant Valley to relieve the Union garrison at Harpers Ferry.

Unfortunately, the operation for General McClellan did not go as planned because he had hoped once he pushed the Confederates away from Turner and Fox's Gaps, he could drive against General Lee's force near the Potomac River at Sharpsburg and possibly trap them while General Franklin destroyed the two Confederate divisions of Major-Generals Lafayette McLaws and Richard Anderson men at Crampton's Gap and in Pleasant Valley behind Maryland Heights. If the plan worked, General McClellan would be successful in preventing Lee's main force from reuniting with the Confederate force under Stonewall Jackson surrounding Harpers Ferry.

The capture of Harpers Ferry was the key to the campaign for General Lee because if Harpers Ferry did not surrender there would be no Battle of Antietam. But in war and battle things do not always go as generals and commanders plan to accomplish. Instead, on September 15, Colonel Dixon S. Miles, the commanding officer at Harpers Ferry and 12,700 Union soldiers surrendered to Stonewall Jackson and his Confederate force. Because of the surrender of Harpers Ferry, Jackson's Confederate force was able to reunite with General Lee's main force and fight along Antietam Creek on September 17, 1862.

I was honored when historical-fiction author Sean Daniels asked me to read the first draft of his manuscript, "Half A Day Late," for historical accuracy and later to write the *Foreword* to his book.

Author Sean Daniels lives in the area of Crampton's Gap where the actual battle took place on September 14, 1862. The area to this day is much like it was in the autumn of 1862. There are no modern-day housing developments and the area is still very rural and populated with farms and rolling hills.

Most historical-fiction authors, who write about a historical event often live or visit the area to familiarize themselves with the terrain, streams, farms, and mountains. This experience always gives them the ability to convey their description and the atmosphere of the area written in their book more precisely and greater visibility to their audience. The famous Civil War author Shelby Foote always visited the battlefields on the month and day to capture the real-life experience of what it was like for civil war soldiers who were involved in that particular event. Most historical-fiction authors rely on primary historical sources and actually only cover a brief period of time that is not captured in the primary text. Sean Daniels has done his homework for his book. In the past, some have been critical of historical-fiction books, but it is an easy way for an audience to learn about a historical event. Sean Daniels has provided such a book for an audience, whose love is historical-fiction novels, and through this avenue they learn about a historical event. Daniels provides such a book with historical accuracy and a story that is weaved throughout about the Battle of Crampton's Gap.

Sean Daniels' novel, "Half A Day Late" is very believable, and a very well written historical-fiction account based on creditable researched material. He uses his characters, who are young farm adults, to reveal the history of what took place the day before and the day of the Battle of Crampton's Gap. His characters come to life by expressing emotions that are so real that an audience can easily identify with any one of them as they read his narrative. Daniels blends historical truth into a narrative where an audience will easily believe that they are actually living through the Battle of Crampton's Gap.

The story characters are good friends, who represent both sides of the warring factions, therefore, the reader learns why the war was being fought and why the story characters were compelled to do what they did during the Battle of Crampton's Gap. While the reader bonds with the characters of the book, Daniels adds a twist to his narrative through a character who you believe that you know but will discover in the end that you really did not know them.

General Franklin's VI Corps arrived in front of Crampton's Gap at noon on September 14, but did not attack the Confederates until 3:00 in the afternoon. Why did it take him three hours to assemble his troops and then attack the Confederate defenders holding the mountain pass? The answer has never been ascertained. Once Crampton's Gap was in Union possession and Confederate forces had scattered after losing the mountain gap why did General Franklin not continue to order the VI Corps forward into Pleasant Valley after the retreating Confederates? He did have a reserve force. Why didn't he use them? Why didn't General Franklin make an attempt to attack General McLaws's Confederate force on September 15, even though he had his reservations about such an attack. It all proved costly because Harpers Ferry surrendered and General Lee was able to reunite his force at Sharpsburg several days later during the fight along Antietam Creek.

There are many "if's" and "why's" that play into the events leading up to and the Battle of Crampton's Gap that historians have never answered. In Sean Daniels' novel, he possibly answers some of those questions of why General Franklin was, **Half A Day Late**.

CW Whitehair,
Summerfield, Florida

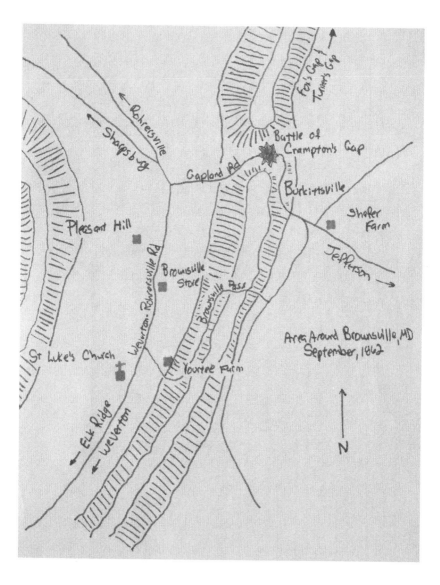

Area around Brownsville, Maryland
September, 1862

CHAPTER I

On Thursday, September 11, 1862, near Brownsville Gap, Jonathan Yourtee's green alfalfa field was dotted with gray uniformed Confederate soldiers camped there. General Lafayette McLaws' Division, under orders from General Robert E. Lee in his Maryland Campaign, had just marched through Brownsville Gap on their way to Maryland Heights to assist in capturing the Federal garrison in Harpers Ferry. Brigadier General Paul J. Semmes in command of a small picket was ordered to remain at the western slope of Brownsville Gap to guard McLaws' rear flank.

A knock was heard at the front door of Mr. and Mrs. Jeremiah Brown's general store. Since Mr. Brown was away in Baltimore conducting business, Mrs. Sally Brown went to the door.

"Who is it?" she asked timidly from behind the heavy door. All day she and her daughter had peeked out windows and spied the Confederate troops filing down the road from Brownsville Gap towards Harpers Ferry. Now a smaller contingent of Rebel soldiers was setting up camp in the field behind them.

"Madam, please allow me to introduce myself. I am Confederate Brigadier General Paul J. Semmes. I apologize in advance for any intrusion, and I want to assure you no harm will come to you or any of your family during our brief stay here in Brownsville," the General practically shouted from the porch outside the bolted door.

"This store and home is owned by my husband, Mr. Jeremiah Brown. Unfortunately he is away on business but he told me under no circumstances to open the door if any soldiers show up here. What is it that you wish, General Semmes?" asked Mrs. Brown.

"We have no wish to disturb you or your family, Mrs. Brown. I only want to ask if it would be all right if my men fill their canteens and water jugs from your spring here and if I could purchase some supplies for my men," asked General Semmes. "Again, I give you my solemn word as a southern gentleman, no harm will come to you or your family," he said.

Mrs. Brown opened the door, taking stock of the large man with a full beard dressed in a rumpled Confederate officer's uniform. "You can help yourself to as much water as you wish. What kind of supplies was you needing, General Semmes?"

"That's mighty kindly of you, Mrs. Brown. As all we have to pay you with is Confederate currency, madam, and who knows how long this war will drag on, I'll just ask for a few pounds of flour and salt pork. I wouldn't want you and your husband to not receive payment for your wares, and we're not asking for charity mam," replied the General. "Also, I would like to warn you to keep your family indoors and away from the windows for the next few days. More than likely there's going to be some action back here in Brownsville Gap, and I wouldn't want any of ya'll to get struck by a stray bullet."

"I appreciate the warning, General. I'll start gathering your supplies," said Mrs. Brown. Right then a beautiful young woman with long brown curls peeked around the kitchen door. "Julia, get back in that kitchen right this minute. Now!" shouted Mrs. Brown. Julia quickly disappeared back into the kitchen. Flustered and with crimson cheeks, Mrs. Brown looked up embarrassedly into General Semmes' eyes. "You'll excuse me and my daughter, General. Neither of us have ever seen a Confederate officer in person before, and as you know, curiosity killed the cat," she said smiling weakly.

"You and your husband should be very proud, Mrs. Brown. Your daughter is a strikingly fine looking young woman. I saw her only for a glimpse, but I have to say she reminds me a lot of my wife back home in Georgia," said General Semmes, tipping his cap as Mrs. Brown gently closed the door.

"Mother, wasn't he just the most handsome man anyone's ever seen around these parts in years? Blonde, wavy curls and eyes the color of blue sky," Julia whispered to Mrs. Brown as she closed the door behind her.

"Get back in that kitchen and stay there. Didn't you just hear him say there's liable to be fighting going on around here soon and here you are practically swooning over the first damn Johnny-Rebel you lay your eyes on!" shouted Mrs. Brown. "Lord help us child, they couldn't have shown up at a worse time, what with your father away at the market in Baltimore through the weekend and you all man crazy, I can't tell if I'm coming or going."

"Oh mother please, I am NOT man crazy. Anyway he already said he has a pretty wife back home, but he looked so tired and worried and he gave us his word he's not going to let any harm come to us. I'm going to make them some pies!" Julia said as she reached for the crock containing the flour.

"Alright, alright, at least it'll give us something to do since we can't go outdoors. But I mean it, Julia, I don't want you going anywhere near those soldiers! What would your father think? He'd probably say makin' pies for the Confederates was aiding the enemy."

The following morning, Friday, a heavy dew lay on the field behind the Brownsville Store. When the sun finally peeked over South Mountain, a delicious aroma wafted through Mr. Yourtee's field near the western base of Brownsville Gap. Small groups of Confederate soldiers stood around campfires with boiling pots of weak coffee.

"I do believe we've all died and gone to heaven," Private Stump said to the men standing around. "If that ain't the smell of apple pie bakin', then I ain't been marching for this Confederate Army for nigh on almost two years now."

"I do believe yer right there, Mr. Stump," said Captain Dunning.

Back in the Brownsville Store's kitchen, Mrs. Brown and Julia had been up since dawn baking apple pies. With the last four just coming out of the oven, that made a total of twenty pies the two of them had made since starting the evening before, right after General Semmes had left them.

"Captain Dunning," said General Semmes, "go down there to the Brown's back porch and see what

Mrs. Brown is waving to us about. And judging by the heavenly aroma coming from their windows, take a couple of men with you."

"Yes sir!" saluted Captain Dunning as he and his troops scurried across the green alfalfa field. As they approached the back door, Mrs. Brown and her daughter Julia came out, each carrying two large baskets filled with hot apple pies.

"Good morning," said Mrs. Brown as the morning sun lit up her smiling face. "Take these back to camp and bring the baskets back 'cause there's plenty more where they come from. Also if you wouldn't mind milking the cows in the barn since we're cooped up here in the house, then there'll be plenty of fresh milk to wash down the pies with." Private Stump couldn't take his eyes off Julia the whole time. Blushing as she handed over the baskets to him, she couldn't help but giggle.

"Julia, that's enough of that!" cried Mrs. Brown. "Get back in the kitchen like I told ya before." Julia grinned and rushed back in the house.

Mrs. Brown and her daughter Julia hand out fresh baked apple pies to Confederate soldiers.

"Thankee, very, very much, Mrs. Brown, and please give our thanks to your daughter too," said Captain Dunning. "A hot, home baked pie with fresh milk for breakfast is the best a humble soldier could ever hope for. I apologize for Private Stump, but honestly mam I don't think he can be rightfully blamed. I expect he nor any of us has ever seen a girl as pretty as your daughter, nor for that matter, ever will again." Now it was Mrs. Brown's turn to blush as she averted her eyes and gave her welcome to the soldiers.

Directly behind Mr. and Mrs. Brown's store, on the other side of the alfalfa field sat Greystone, the Yourtee family home. The Yourtees were one of the first families to settle in Pleasant Valley back in the 1700's, and they owned the entire hundred-acre farm that was now serving as a base camp for General Semmes and his Confederate soldiers.

"What is Mrs. Brown and her silly daughter up to out there, Daniel?" asked Jonathan Yourtee, leaning behind his son Daniel looking out a window of Greystone across the alfalfa field.

"Looks like they're handing out fresh pies to them darn Rebels, father," replied his son.

"Well, if that don't beat all," said Mr. Yourtee, slapping his hand on his knee. "Wait until Jeremiah Brown hears about this. "

Daniel stood scratching the short scrubble of a beard on his chin. He had a date to go to the Friday night dance over in Rohrersville with Julia Brown, but now he was wondering if there would still be a dance tonight, what with Rebels camped right here in our fields in Pleasant Valley.

"I already know what you're thinking too," said Mr. Yourtee. "You won't be going to any dances or any other shenanigans tonight either. Not as long as we've got a war going on right here in our backyards, you ain't. Now get upstairs and get all them rifles and pistols loaded like I asked you to, boy."

"Aw father, you know how long I've been after Miss Brown to go to the dance with me, and now here she finally said 'yes' and I can't go," whined Daniel as he started up the stairs.

Alice Yourtee put her hand on her husband's shoulder. "Of course you're right dear. We can't have the children running around after dark with all these soldiers camped all over, but Daniel's so disappointed. He's been looking forward to this night for almost a month now," she said.

"It can't be helped, Alice. There'll come another day. But if you asked me, the boy will be better off the farther away from that Brown girl as he can get. She ain't nothing but trouble. She's got every young feller in this valley's head turned to where ain't none of 'em can see straight any more," Mr. Yourtee said. "Anyway, we got more to worry about than them two love birds. I'm going to ride up to Crampton's Gap and have a little talk with the neighbors up there. See if I can't find out what the dickens is going on around here. Make sure Daniel has all the weapons and shells all ready in case it comes down to havin' to use 'em. Lock all the doors behind me and don't open 'em 'til I get back. I won't be gone long. Be back 'fore dark anyway."

"Please be careful, Jonathan," said Mrs. Yourtee. She closed the door behind her husband and turned the deadbolt, locking it firmly in place. Alice Yourtee watched her husband lead his horse from the barn, mount it and trot down the road towards Rohrersville Pike. When he had almost disappeared from view, she turned and walked up the stairs to go and see if she could console her son.

General Semmes and Captain Dunning washed down the last couple of bites of pie with fresh milk, cleared the table in front of them and unrolled a map of South Mountain. Sipping their hot weak coffee (actually more chicory root than coffee, but it was the best the Rebels could scrape up these days) the two officers traced the route that they and General McLaws had just taken through Brownsville Pass (it was noted on the map that this pass was also sometimes referred to as Burkittsville Pass). They also noticed another pass on the map,

Crampton's Gap, not quite a mile to the north of there, where another road wound up over the mountain coming west out of Burkittsville.

"Do you suppose it's possible, Captain Dunning, that the Union forces might try to cross South Mountain by way of this other pass, instead of through here like we did?" asked General Semmes, pointing on the map to Crampton's Gap.

"Anything's possible, at least in this crazy war so far. But why would the Federals want to delay their arrival in Harpers Ferry by taking a more northern route? It wouldn't make sense in my mind, General," replied Captain Dunning.

"Well, we'll have to make sure our scouts at the top of Brownsville Pass keep a sharp lookout. You can see for miles to the east from there so we should have plenty of notice when they get here," said General Semmes. "And remember, we've got General Mahone with his three regiments of infantry, General Cobb's Georgian brigade, and Colonel Munford's small detachment of cavalry already guarding Crampton's Gap. Let's you and me and some officers take a ride up to the top of the mountain and take another look around this morning. While General Semmes rolled up his map, he looked in the direction of the Yourtee home and said, "Captain, see that man riding his horse away from the gray stone house there. Better send a few men after him, find out who he is and what he's up to?"

"Yes sir, right away, sir," replied Captain Dunning, saluting the General as he left the command tent."

Mrs. Yourtee didn't notice the group of three Rebel soldiers on horseback that took off in a gallop after her husband down the road to Rohrersville Pike. Jonathan Yourtee hadn't gone far when the three soldiers on horseback overtook him on the road towards Rohrersville.

"Halt right there, sir!" shouted one of the young soldiers, pointing a loaded pistol in Mr. Yourtee's direction. He pulled on the reins of his horse and turned to face the soldiers.

"What's the trouble here?" asked Mr. Yourtee. "And I'd take it kindly if you put that pistol away, young man, before someone gets hurt," he said to the young soldier, noticing he couldn't be much older than his son Daniel, back at Greystone.

"Sorry, sir, holstering his pistol," sheepishly replied the young soldier. "We've got orders to question you. Please state your name and business out here on this road today."

Mr. Yourtee was not used to being questioned, especially while still on his own property. He couldn't decide whether to be angry or just annoyed, but looking in the young soldier's eyes he saw the same fear he'd seen in Daniel's eyes earlier that morning. "My name is Jonathan Yourtee and I own this farm that you soldiers are camped on right now. I'm on my way to a neighbor's house to check on them. Now I know you have your orders but folks here in the valley don't ride up on one another pointing pistols in their faces."

"My apologies, Mr. Yourtee. We saw you leave from that gray stone farmhouse back there. Our officers have instructed us to tell you that we wish you nor your family any harm, but our orders are to escort you back to your house where we would ask you to remain. We expect Federal troops to try and pass through this valley, possibly within the next couple of days, so with that said we're asking everyone to stay in their homes until this action is over," said the young soldier.

"Well, we'll see about that!" Mr. Yourtee grumbled angrily. Looking from face to face of the three young Rebels, he calmed himself and continued, "I guess orders are orders, young man. I'll do as I'm asked. You'll get no trouble from me as long as you don't stick any more pistols in my face." The three soldiers fell in line behind him and escorted him back to his barn where he dismounted and put his horse away and walked back to the porch of Greystone. Before entering he turned and tipped his hat to the departing soldiers. Jonathan Yourtee had read plenty of newspaper reports of Confederates looting of civilians. His own cousin near Baltimore had had his barn burned and lost most of a year's crop of hay. He thought to himself that at least these soldiers had given their officers' word that no harm would come to him or his family if they cooperated with their orders. Still, it was a sad day when a man couldn't leave his own farm and ride over to check on his neighbor. Scratching his forehead, he knew all along that there'd come a day when Lincoln wouldn't be able to keep this war on the Virginia side of the Potomac River. Now that day was here.

As Jonathan was turning the key in the lock to his kitchen door, his wife and son were just returning from upstairs. The room that was now the kitchen in Greystone was once a fort where the early settlers fought off the Indians in these parts. The last thing he wanted to see happen was to let Greystone get burned by Confederate soldiers.

"Jonathan, what are you doing back so soon? You can't have rode all the way to Crampton Gap and returned," said Alice Yourtee to her husband.

"No, I didn't even get out of sight before some Rebel soldiers chased me down and stuck a pistol in

17

my face. But don't worry. They gave their officers' word that no harm would come to any of us as long as we stay put in the house here," replied Mr. Yourtee, still scratching his head.

"Oh dear!" cried Mrs. Yourtee, hugging her husband and burying her tear-strewn face in his chest. "How long are we going to be held captive in our own homes?"

"Pray, I don't know, Alice, and the Rebels don't know either. But if I was a betting man, I'd say it ain't gonna be too long. These boys are fixin' for a fight for this mountain behind us here. They said they expected the Union troops to be coming this way en route to Harpers Ferry any day now to try and provide reinforcements to the Federal garrison there. Best thing for us to do is just sit tight, keep away from the windows and wait it out," said Mr. Yourtee. "I've met a few southern gentlemen in my day and they all looked like men that would stand by their word. We don't want Greystone ending up burned to the ground like I read the Confederates did over in Virginia last year."

"Well, since we're all stuck here just waiting around. I've got an idea. Why don't we hold a fried chicken supper followed by a little dancing tomorrow night. I'm sure the officers could use a break from all this dreary fighting and killing, and certainly the Federals won't be coming in the dark," said Alice wiping a tear and smiling up into her husband's eyes.

Jonathan Yourtee smiled back into his wife's eyes and gently lifted her chin to his and kissed her lightly on the lips. "That sounds like the best idea I've heard all day Alice. After lunch I'll walk down to their camp and talk it over with the officers. I can't think of any better way to stay off the bad side of these Rebs, then to fill up their bellies with some of your home made fried chicken. I'll break out a couple jugs of cider from the cellar too, might loosen them up a little bit."

"Oh goodie! A dance on Saturday night," piped up their son Daniel. "Can we invite the Browns mother? Please, please," begged Daniel.

Still smiling at each other, Mr. and Mrs. Yourtee both turned facing towards their son. Mr. Yourtee couldn't help but think at that moment of the young Rebel soldier he had just encountered out on the road and how he and Daniel were about the same age. Placing his hand on his son's shoulder and looking fondly down into his face, Mr. Yourtee said, "that will be fine, Daniel. I'll mention it to the officers this afternoon."

Later that day, Mr. Yourtee watched from out of his window in Greystone a group of Rebel officers return down Brownsville Pass on horseback. As he watched the officers' horses carefully pick their way through the rocky pass, he reflected on all he and his family had to be thankful for. His grandparents had settled here in Pleasant Valley more than a hundred years ago. They had hauled gray rocks from the creek beds with mule-drawn wagons and built the gray stone mansion now named Greystone before he was born. They had cleared the forest and plowed the fields where now the fresh green alfalfa grew. As if waking from a dream, Jonathan took up his makeshift white flag and waving it as he walked, approached the Confederates command tent. After introducing himself to General Semmes and his officers, it didn't take very long to convince them to join the Yourtees on Saturday evening for a fried chicken supper followed by a dance. Mr. Yourtee gave them the names of the local families to be sure to invite, not only to ensure to have some female partners to dance with, but also to be sure Tommy Krause showed up with his fiddle, because their couldn't be a local dance in Brownsville without Tommy's fiddle playing.

CHAPTER II

Six days earlier, on September 6, 1862 President Abraham Lincoln issued orders naming Major General George B. McClellan to the command of the newly formed Army of the Potomac. When the soldiers received the news, cheers were raised and hats flew in the air as "Little Mac," as he had become fondly known was well liked amongst the troops.

Just forty-eight hours before McClellan had received his new command, the recently victorious Confederate Army of Northern Virginia now led by General Robert E. Lee, had crossed the Potomac, launching its first invasion in Northern territory. After marching through Frederick, Maryland, General Lee continued westward looking to capture the Federal garrisons at Harpers Ferry and Martinsburg, Virginia, thereby securing his lines of communication from the west. In order for Lee to be successful, his army would also need to hold the passes on South Mountain.

The Union Army of the Potomac began marching west from Washington. General McClellan divided his army into three wings. Led by General Burnside, the right wing was made up of the First and Ninth Corps. The center wing, which would be held in reserve for the upcoming operation, was commanded by General Sumner. The Sixth Corps and Major General Darius Couch's division from the Fourth Corps comprised the left wing under the command of General William B. Franklin.

On Saturday afternoon, September 13th, 1862...
"in a meadow just east of Frederick, an area recently occupied by the Army of Northern Virginia, a corporal of the Twenty-seventh Indiana Infantry found a copy of Lee's Special Orders Number 191, spelling out the current operations of the Army of Northern Virginia," wrapped around a couple of *cigars.* 1

1 quote from *First to Last: The Life of Major General William B. Franklin by Mark A. Snell,* Page 173

When McClellan received this copy of Lee's orders, he quickly made plans to take advantage of Lee's bold plan to divide his army in enemy territory.

At 6:20P.M. Saturday evening, September 13th, the "Young Napoleon," General McClellan, sent specific orders to General Franklin in which he spelled out his plan to "cut the enemy in two and beat him in detail." Franklin's Sixth Corps were ordered to seize Crampton's Gap. From his headquarters, on the east side of Catoctin Mountain, they were ordered to march through the village of Jefferson, Maryland, on the way to Burkittsville at the eastern base of South Mountain. McClellan's orders stated, "If this pass is not occupied by the enemy, seize it as soon as practicable and debouch upon Rohrersville in order to cut off or destroy McLaws' command."

Confederate General Lafayette McLaws commanded a division that was in the area of Maryland Heights, a few miles south of Crampton's

Gap, which overlooked the town of Harpers Ferry on the eastern side of the Potomac River. McLaws' division was part of a three-pronged attack on the federal garrison at Harpers Ferry under the overall command of Stonewall Jackson.

Furthermore, McClellan's orders compelled Franklin to "Having gained the pass, (Crampton's Gap was also referred to as Crampton's Pass), your duty will be to cut off, destroy, or capture McLaws' command and relieve Colonel Miles." (Miles was the Federal commander of the Harpers Ferry garrison.) General McClellan knew that Franklin's mission was vital to the overall success of his plan. He went on to say to his old friend, "I ask of you at this important moment all your intellect & the utmost activity a general can exercise."

William B. Franklin had graduated from the United States Military Academy first in his class in 1843. An engineer before the outbreak of the Civil War, he supervised the construction of the U.S. Capitol Dome and in March 1861 was the supervising architect of the new U.S. Treasury building in Washington. Before that he was the supervisor of the Lighthouse Board, responsible for the building of lighthouses across the country. In March 1862, Franklin was appointed to lead the Sixth Corps, which he led in the Virginia Peninsula Campaign. A sign that he was growing weary of this war was evidenced by the conclusion of a letter he penned to his wife Anna the day before on September 12th. "When will the time come when we can go somewhere when there will be no more wars, and nothing but peace and quiet? I would willingly live on five hundred dollars a year to be in quiet again. But God's will be done."

Saturday night, September 13th, at 10:00 P.M, Franklin acknowledged receipt of McClellan's orders and replied, "I have received your orders, understand them, and will do my best to carry them out. My command will commence its movement at 5 ½ A.M."

CHAPTER III

Everything was set for the fried chicken supper and dance back in Brownsville at Greystone. Another tawny Saturday evening in September unfolded at the base of South Mountain. Rustic tables covered with freshly laundered, white embroidered tablecloths were spread around the lawn outside the Yourtee's front porch. Baskets of hot buttery biscuits mixed with platters of crisp Maryland fried chicken filled the tabletops. Another table decorated with white frills was loaded with pies, cakes, and plates of cookies that the neighbors had contributed. Inside the house, the large table had been moved to the far end of the dining room. An ornate punch bowl surrounded by crystal punch glasses was placed in the middle of the table on top of a white, crocheted tablecloth. The rug in the dining room had been rolled up and stowed behind the table to make room for the dancing.

Confederate General Paul J. Semmes and his officers had taken advantage of the clear spring water bubbling out of the ground near the rear of the Brownsville Store to clean their uniforms and wash up and shave. Promptly at six sharp they arrived at Greystone and made their greetings to the Yourtee family. Although still a ragtag looking group of soldiers in their tattered gray Confederate uniforms, they were now at least presentable. They found a whirlwind of activity. Mrs. Brown and her daughter, the stunning Julia, were still carrying platters of fried chicken and baskets of buttered biscuits from the kitchen out to the tables outside. Standing gathered around the tables, others sitting in chairs were the twenty some residents of the little farming village of Brownsville. Some of the men were clustered under a shady oak tree smoking their pipes while the women were still unloading their baskets of desserts. Some boys had gathered at the edge of the yard and were busily playing a game of mumblety-peg. A group of girls were in the middle of ring-around-the-rosy. Under a maple tree at the corner of the porch, Daniel

Yourtee rolled up a keg of cool cider he had just brought from the cellar of Greystone.

"Welcome to a little Pleasant Valley hospitality," said Jonathan Yourtee, extending his hand to General Semmes.

"Thank you, sir. My men and I are honored to accept. It's not often that humble soldiers are able to take even a short break from this war, and especially for such a special treat as this," replied the General.

"Well, come on everyone. Let's bow our heads and thank our Maker for this food we're about to eat," said Mr. Yourtee. He bowed his head and closed his eyes and prayed, "Heavenly Father, giver of all great gifts, grant one more we beseech Thee, that of a grateful heart." Then opening his eyes he said, "Alright, come on and dig in every one. Eat as much as you want. There's more chicken frying in the kitchen and biscuits in the oven."

Tommy Krause, the fiddle player, arrived on horseback, escorted by Captain Dunning over Brownsville Pass from his home in Burkittsville.

True to his word, General Semmes had provided an escort for Tommy so that there would be certain to be music for the dancing later that evening. He made his greetings, and thanks to General Semmes and his officers and the folks starting to fill their plates, and then excused himself to go into the kitchen and pay his respects to Mrs. Yourtee and the womenfolk. Daniel Yourtee wasn't the only young man in Pleasant Valley who had had his eye on Julia Brown over the years, so Tommy was anxious to see Julia again and say hello.

"Well, well, well, look here ladies, "said Mrs. Brown. "If it's not the handsomest bachelor in Pleasant Valley arrived. Tommy Krause has brought his fiddle to entertain us this evening."

Tommy's cheeks were flushed crimson with embarrassment but he smiled, making his way around the kitchen, hugging and kissing Mrs. Brown and the other women who stopped cooking for a moment, wiping their hands on their aprons. Julia Brown, who had been talking with Mr. Yourtee, turned towards Tommy as he made his way across the room. Now it was her turn to get the color up in her cheeks. She hadn't seen Tommy since that day a few weeks ago down at the swimming hole at the bend in Antietam Creek where she had allowed him to kiss her when the rest of the kids had swam around the bend.

Tommy took her hands in his, gave them a little squeeze and gave her a quick peck on the neck and said, "Julia Brown, I do declare, you get lovelier every time I see you." At that moment Jonathan Yourtee, gently guiding Tommy towards the parlor, said, "Come Tommy, I've been wanting to show you my great grandfather's fiddle we found while cleaning out the attic the other day. It's just here in the parlor closet."

Mr. Yourtee and Tommy disappeared through the parlor door. "Why Mr. Yourtee, you never told me your great grandfather played the fiddle," Tommy said.

"Shhhh, listen Tommy, we may not have much time before one of those Confederate officers come looking for us," whispered Mr. Yourtee. "Did you notice how many Confederate troops were in Brownsville Pass when you come through there just now?

"Well as a matter of fact, sir, I did notice, and there were a lot. They got infantry at the bottom of the mountain, then with rows of cavalry behind them, and then a little further up the mountain they've got a row of big cannons and other artillery set up. It's almost like they're expecting to ambush those Federals if they're fixing to march through Brownsville," replied Tommy.

"That's what I figured," said Mr. Yourtee. "Several Rebel divisions marched through here and headed south towards Harpers Ferry a couple of days ago, and I reckon these troops that are here now have been left behind to guard their rear, 'cause they already told me they're expecting action in this pass when the Federals show up here any day now. So listen, you got to figure out a way to get them to escort you back home tonight by way of Crampton's Pass so you can see how many rebels are over there? Then you let your pa know which pass is the least defended and have him get word to the Union commanders, see? They got everyone over here in Brownsville kept hostage in our homes, so you're our only chance."

"You can count on me, Mr. Yourtee, and I know just how we'll do it. There ain't a man that's still got blood flowing through his veins that could resist those long batting eyelashes of Julia Brown's," said Tommy. "I'll get her to cozy up to Captain Dunning and convince him to let me take some of her sewing back to her cousin, Doris, over on Whipp's Ravine. Don't you worry, Mr. Yourtee. We'll pull this off and those Rebels won't suspect a thing."

"Good, that's real good, Tommy. I always knew you had a smart head on your shoulders. Well, I guess we better get on back out there and mingle with the enemy before they notice we've been missing," said Jonathan Yourtee, winking to Tommy as he clasped his shoulder.

Another table had been set up under a shade tree with buckets of warm water, soap, and clean towels for folks to wash their hands when they finished eating to get ready for the dance. Tommy Krause knew that once the dance started, he'd be too busy to get a word in with Julia so when he saw her approaching the washing table he joined her.

"Good evening, Julia, it's good to see you tonight. I need a word with you, in private, before the dance gets started," Tommy whispered in her ear.

Julia started and turned sharply to face him. "Well, Tommy Krause, you mind your manners," she said. "Just because I let you kiss me down at the creek..."

"Shhhh," whispered Tommy, "this is serious. Meet me in the Yourtee's parlor, I'll explain later."

Daniel Yourtee hadn't taken his eyes off Julia all evening, and he didn't miss seeing Tommy Krause whispering in her ear. As soon as Tommy headed towards the Yourtee's back porch he confronted Julia on the lawn.

"Hello, Julia," said Daniel. "I thought we had a date tonight? Or are you going to spoil it by sneaking off with Tommy again?"

"Oh Daniel, I do believe you're jealous," replied Julia, taking Daniel's hands into hers. "I don't know what I'm going to do with you," she said smiling sweetly up into Daniel's eyes. "I promised I'd dance with you and I will, but only if you promise to behave yourself this evening. With all these Rebel soldiers all over the place, Mother insisted I be on my best behavior and I think that goes for all of us. I'll see you on the dance floor. Now I've got to go help the other women clean up the kitchen," said Julia as she headed towards Greystone.

While the other women were busy talking and washing the dishes, Julia slipped through the parlor door to find Tommy waiting on the other side.

"This better not be another one of your little tricks, Tommy Krause."

Tommy put his fingers on Julia's lips and said, "Shhh, listen, I don't have much time. I need to get out to the dance and start warming up before those Rebs get suspicious. Mr. Yourtee wants me to go home by way of Crampton Pass so I can get a count of how many Confederates are guarding that pass and tell my pa, so he can warn the Federals to take the least defended pass when they march west towards Maryland Heights. "

"So what does that have to do with me?" asked Julia.

"We need you to convince Captain Dunning who escorted me over here to escort me that way back home tonight. Tell him you've got some sewing that you've been trying to get to your cousin Doris, and because everyone in Brownsville's been kept cooped up in their houses, you haven't been able to go visit her," quickly whispered Tommy.

"But what if he doesn't agree to it?" asked Julia.

"Use your charm, Julia, do whatever it takes. You'll be fine," replied Tommy, holding Julia's chin and kissing her lightly on her forehead.

Julia smiled back up at Tommy. "I just hope that Daniel Yourtee doesn't cause a scene. You know how jealous he gets," she replied.

"That's what you get for leading him on in the first place. I told you before. You need to stop fooling with that young boy before he gets hurt," said Tommy. "You can handle Daniel, I've got to go now. Good luck."

Tommy fiddles the tunes for the dance at Greystone.

On one wall in the dining room underneath the portrait of Jonathan Yourtee's father, Samuel Yourtee, was a row of chairs where the young ladies sat waiting to be asked to dance. One of these young ladies was Rebecca Burgard who lived on the western side of the Weverton-Rohersville Road in a large brick home that was known in the valley as Pleasant Hill. Rebecca was a shy but beautiful young woman who, like the others had grown up here in Pleasant Valley, had only strayed from these hills once. When she was fifteen her father had taken her to visit their aunts and uncles in Georgia. Now, because of that visit, folks in the valley began to suspect that Jacob Burgard was a Confederate sympathizer. And because of that, none of the local boys had asked her to dance. Rebecca had become accustomed to this situation. She was a wallflower and she knew it, but it didn't make her very happy. Julia Brown, on the other hand, had scarcely a minute to sit down the entire evening. From the very beginning when Tommy Krause's fiddle struck up the notes of the first waltz and Daniel Yourtee whisked her onto the dance floor, young man after young man cut in and kept her on her feet. To Julia's dismay though, the local boys had kept her completely away from any of the young Confederate officers, and she was becoming desperate to somehow speak to Captain Dunning without raising suspicions.

Captain Dunning and the other Confederate officers were spellbound by Julia Brown's stunning good looks and soon became aware that the local men were monopolizing her company. But, alas, they were guests and bound by the honor of southern gentlemen to not create a scene. Out of the corner of his eye, Captain Dunning spied the young red-haired Rebecca sitting all alone along the wall. Unlike Julia and the other young women there tonight, whose hair was worn long, Rebecca's hair was cropped short, barely reaching her shoulders. Bowing in front of her, Captain Dunning said, "Please allow me to introduce myself, madam, I am Captain George Dunning from the 10th Georgia regiment. Would you do me the honor of dancing with me?"

"Why of course, Captain, I would be happy to," said Rebecca. The couple danced around and round. As they danced the Captain whispered to Rebecca, "I couldn't help but notice that your hair is cut short, while most of the other girls wear their hair long."

Shyly she whispered back, "That's true, Captain. You see, I must admit I'm a bit of a tomboy. I like to fish and hunt and work the fields. Why, do you know I can shoot a rifle every bit as good as any of my brothers."

"Is that right?" replied the Captain.

"Yes, sir, when my father took us to visit our family in Georgia, I was the only one to kill a deer in the woods on their plantation outside of Athens," said Rebecca.

"You have family in Georgia. Why that's where I'm from," said Captain Dunning, smiling down into Rebecca's upturned face. "What's your family's surname, if I may be so bold as to ask?"

"It's really Beauregard, but Daddy changed it to Burgard when we bought our farm here in Maryland. We still have three slaves that we brought with us from Georgia: Billy and Bessie, and their fifteen year-old son, Otis. Billy and Bessie are as old as Mommy and Daddy. Billy and Otis help with the farm chores, and Bessie was my nanny when I was growing up, and she's just the best cook and housekeeper in the whole world. We wouldn't know how to get along without them, to be truthful, Captain. And I taught Otis to read and write," said Rebecca.

"And your neighbors here in Maryland don't mind you keeping slaves?" asked the Captain.

"Oh, we don't care what the neighbors think. Father said not to pay any attention to them."

Julia Brown knew it would be a bold move, but she could see no other way to get Captain Dunning's ear. She whispered to Daniel, "Excuse me a minute, Daniel," and before he even knew what was happening, Julia stepped between Captain Dunning and Rebecca and cut in on her. It was an extremely embarrassing moment. While Captain Dunning and Julia danced away, Daniel and Rebecca were left standing next to each other out on the dance floor. Daniel, only to stave off his embarrassment, immediately took Rebecca's hand in his and continued to dance. Poor Rebecca thought she was about to faint from the shock but recovered in Daniel's arms.

"I swear, Rebecca. I don't know what's got into Julia's head this evening," Daniel said softly in Rebecca's ear.

"Oh, Captain Dunning. Please excuse my behavior, but I declare I believe these country boys were going to dance me right off my feet without ever giving any of you handsome officers even a chance," whispered Julia in the Captain's ear.

The Captain chuckled with delight. "You're a spry little filly. I'll give you that," Captain Dunning replied.

"These young fellers here in Pleasant valley will have many more dances with me. I thought I'd die if I didn't get a chance to dance with you this evening, but to tell the truth they've kept me going all night without a break. Would you mind when this dance is over to get us something to drink and perhaps we could go out on the porch where it's quiet and rest a minute. I absolutely have to get out of these pointed shoes, even if it's only for a minute," said Julia.

"Why of course, Miss Brown. But do you think there'll be a scene?" asked the Captain. "Especially with Mr. Yourtee's young son that you so unceremoniously deserted out on the dance floor."

"Oh, don't worry about Daniel, Captain. We've grown up together since we were babies. And anyway he and Rebecca seem to be enjoying themselves now," responded Julia.

As soon as the music stopped, Captain Dunning ladled out two glasses of punch, handing one of them to Julia. Taking her arm, they walked out on to the Yourtee's back porch. Daniel started to go after them but was stopped when his father stepped in front of him.

"But father, did you see what she did?" pleaded Daniel incredulously. "She ought to be spanked!"

"Not now, son. Get hold of yourself. You're acting like an ass," Mr. Yourtee quietly said to Daniel. "Go get Rebecca a glass of punch and pretend like nothing ever happened. I'll explain later."

Daniel recoiled from his father's grasp, now even more confused than before. He couldn't recall the last time he'd ever heard his father utter a curse word, and hadn't everyone seen what Julia had done to him out on the dance floor; he would be the laughing stock of Pleasant Valley. His face turned beet-red, but he obeyed his father and quietly stepped over to the punch table and poured himself and Rebecca a glass.

Out on the back porch swing, Captain Dunning and Julia sat drinking their punch. Julia had kicked off her dancing shoes and was looking up in to the Captain's handsome face.

"You must miss your wife something terrible, Captain Dunning," said Julia. "Seems like this war's gone on ever so long."

"I do miss her deeply, Miss Brown, especially on these very rare occasions when we officers get an opportunity to enjoy the company of fair ladies like yourself. And you may not believe this, but I have a new son that I've not even seen yet," said Captain Dunning grinning broadly.

"That's wonderful!" cried Julia. "I mean it's wonderful you have a son, not that you haven't been able to see him of course. You might not expect it of me, but I sew and make clothes for babies and children to bring in a little extra money. Lord knows with this war and times being tough, we all have to pitch in and do what we can. Yesterday I finished making a sleeper that I bet would fit your son perfectly. Please let me make a gift of it to you to send home for him. It would mean so much to me."

"Oh no, I couldn't let you do that, Miss Brown," said the Captain.

"No, but I insist!" Julia stood up and grabbed the Captain's hand, pulling him off the swing. "Come, walk me down to my house. It was getting stuffy in there anyway and I could use a little fresh air. It'll only take a second to run in and grab it off the top of my sewing basket. Please, Captain Dunning, it would please me so."

"Very well then, never let it be said that a gentleman in the Dunning family would go against a lady's wishes," said Captain Dunning. The Captain, taking Julia's elbow, helped her down the porch stairs, and they started walking down the lawn of Greystone towards Brownsville Store. It was a starry night in Brownsville, and the lightening bugs were in full bloom. "I don't know how I'll be able to repay you for the kind favor, Miss Brown. We more than likely will be leaving tomorrow, and all I have is Confederate currency, which won't buy much in these parts."

"It's a gift, Captain Dunning. Therefore, it requires no payment. But there is one thing you could do, if you'd be so kind. You see, my cousin

Doris over on Whipp's Ravine and I work together. I make the clothes and she embroiders them, but with everyone kept locked up in their houses I haven't been able to get the latest batch of baby clothes I've made over to her, and we're falling behind on our orders."

"Whipp's Ravine is just up the road a mile on Crampton's Pass if I'm not mistaken," said Captain Dunning. "I could have that fiddler drop it off to her when I escort him back to Burkittsville tonight after the dance."

"Would you do that for me?" asked Julia, batting her eyelashes, looking up into the Captain's blue eyes. "That would be absolutely wonderful."

"Of course, I would consider it a privilege to assist a couple of young ladies who are making an honest effort to help themselves in war time," said Captain Dunning.

When the two of them returned to Greystone, Captain Dunning excused himself to stow the sleeper wrapped in a white silk scarf that Julia had given him, in his field pack.

"You better go on in, Miss Brown," said the Captain, letting loose of her elbow. "It might not be best if we return together."

"Of course Captain, and thank you again for helping with our little sewing mission. I better find Daniel and make up that dance to him before he calls out the cavalry and spoils this lovely evening," said Julia laughing, and now with all the color returned to her face.

Later that evening, while Captain Dunning was escorting Tommy Krause home to Burkittsville by way of Crampton's Gap, General Semmes and Jonathan Yourtee enjoyed cigars and a glass of sherry under the stars in the backyard of Greystone.

CHAPTER IV

Sunday morning, September 14, 1862, another clear day arose in Pleasant Valley. Early that morning, Confederate Major General J.E.B. Stuart and his cavalry were already on the move en route to Harpers Ferry. At the western base of South Mountain on Gapland Road, less than a mile west of Crampton Pass, Stuart met with Brigadier General Wade Hampton and Colonel Thomas Munford whose cavalries were guarding Crampton Pass. General Stuart decided to take Hampton's cavalry with him to Harpers Ferry to help with the Confederate seizure of the Federal garrison there. That left Colonel Munford with only the 2nd and 12th Virginia Cavalry, fewer than three hundred troopers, to guard any potential Federal advance through Crampton Pass.

Late that morning, from the peak of Crampton's Gap, Colonel Munford sighted a large Federal force approaching his position from the east. Less than a mile to the south from his position at the crest of

Brownsville Pass, Brigadier General Paul Semmes also watched the three long blue columns moving closer. In order to reinforce Munford's line, Semmes decided to send to Crampton's Gap, Colonel William A. Parham's undersized brigade, the 6th, 12th, and 16th Virginia Infantry regiments and the Portsmouth Light Artillery, as well as the 10th Georgia Infantry from his own brigade. All told, there were still only roughly eight hundred Confederate muskets in place to defend a Federal advance on Crampton's Gap. As Captain Dunning, assigned to General Semmes' 10th Georgia Infantry, fell in line to depart Brownsville, he spotted Julia Brown waving from the back porch of the Brownsville Store. He lifted his field pack from the ground and, putting it on his back, grinned and waved back.

General Semmes had steadfastly chosen to remain in Brownsville, convinced that any Federal thrust would follow the same route as McLaws had taken. Therefore, he kept his own, much larger brigade with him. He also retained the six-gun battery of Captain Basil Manly's 1st North Carolina Artillery and one gun each from the Richmond (Virginia) Fayette Artillery and the Magruder (Virginia) Light Artillery.

CHAPTER V

Major General J.E.B. Stuart wasn't the only one up early on that bright Sunday September morning. Union Major General William B. Franklin's VI Division, numbering 12,800 men, was on the march westward at daybreak. However, the advantage gained by getting on the move so early was soon squandered. After crossing Catoctin Mountain by way of Mountville Pass, Franklin stopped after about three miles, on the other side of Jefferson. Here he waited for Couch's IV Division to catch up and join him. Not only was this a serious delay costing the Federal forces several hours but it also was explicitly against General McClellan's orders. Finally by around 10 A.M. when Franklin received word that Couch's Division was still at least a couple of hours away, he proceeded to march west to Burkittsville.

Advancing across the rolling hillside and despite having to ford several streams Franklin's VI Division made relatively good time. As commander of the Second Brigade of Franklin's First Division, Colonel Joseph J. Bartlett and the 96th Pennsylvania Infantry were at the front of the VI Division as they continued marching west towards Burkittsville.

Colonel Bartlett was a volunteer soldier and had no formal military training, but despite that he had risen through the ranks and was respected by his men. At noon, when the 96th Pennsylvania Infantry turned left into Distillery Lane about a quarter mile east of Burkittsville, Colonel Bartlett, using his men as skirmishers, crossed a fence line into a field behind the town. Within minutes Confederate artillery fire from Brownsville Pass forced the Federals back. Now it was the Confederate skirmishers' turn as they briefly advanced into the village only to be driven back up to the base of South Mountain by Bartlett's men. Then Colonel Bartlett ordered the rest of his brigade over to a position on the right side of the village, concealing them from the enemy and protecting them from the Confederate artillery fire coming from Brownsville Pass.

By that time the rest of Franklin's VI Division had arrived and began cooking their rations for lunch. Colonel Bartlett had received orders to report to headquarters that had been established at Martin T. Shafer's farm on the east side of Burkittsville, using the buildings of the village to shield them from Confederate artillery fire. As he proceeded east on Main Street a man opened the front door of his house and approached him.

"Sir, excuse me, sir, can I speak to you for a minute?" asked Richard Krause of the Union Colonel.

"Oh, sorry, you startled me," replied Colonel Bartlett. "What is it? I've been summoned back to headquarters, and I'm on my way there now, so I must ask you to be brief sir."

"Sir, my name is Richard Krause and I live here in Burkittsville and I'm proud to say that I support President Lincoln and everything he and your troops are doing to preserve this great Union and this great country, the United States of America. I thought you might be interested in knowing some intelligence about the enemy you're facing there on South Mountain," said Mr. Krause.

"Indeed, indeed I would, sir," replied Colonel Bartlett. "It's a pleasure to meet you, I'm Colonel Joseph J. Bartlett of the Federal VI Corps. What can you tell me about those Confederates lodged in the woods there?"

"Well Colonel, my son Tommy was playing his fiddle at a dance over there at the Yourtee farm in Brownsville last night. They sent an official escort to come get him and to bring him back home. Most folks around here use Brownsville Pass that runs to the south of town, as it's the most direct route across South Mountain and brings you out almost a mile south over in Pleasant Valley. That's the way all them Confederates took when they marched through here back on Thursday. There's a whole big camp of them Rebels perched at the western base of South Mountain as soon as you come through Brownsville Pass. Tommy and his girl, Miss Julia Brown, came up with a scheme to get them to escort him home last night over Crampton's Gap so he could spy on how many Rebels were on Gapland Road. And I got to tell you there ain't even a quarter as many Rebels guarding that pass as there are waiting for you Bluecoats over on Brownsville Pass," said Mr. Krause.

"Is that so? Well how do I know I can trust you and you're not a secessionist setting us up for a trap?" asked the Colonel.

"Do you think I'd be out here in the street taking a chance on getting a bullet from one of you skirmishers running back and forth all through town, just to make up some cock and bull story," replied Richard Krause. "Didn't you notice when you arrived where all the heavy artillery was coming from? It was from the southern end of town on the road over to Brownsville. I swear as God is my Maker that this is the truth, sir, and if you Yankees want to get over South Mountain in one piece, you'll attack them on the road on the right here going over Crampton's Gap."

"Guess you got a point there. Well, I thank you, sir, for the information, thank you very much," said

Colonel Bartlett warmly shaking Mr. Krause's hand. "I got to run now before the General thinks I got killed by a damn Rebel sniper. It was a pleasure to meet you and Good bye, sir."

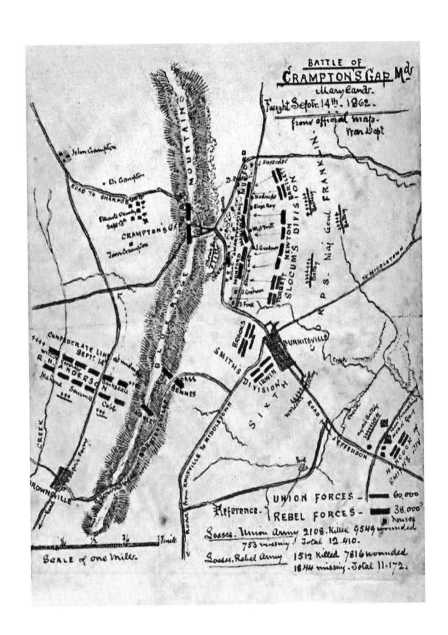

The Battle of Crampton's Gap

CHAPTER VI

Major General William B. Franklin had set up headquarters of his VI Corps on the farm of Martin T. Shafer just outside on the eastern side of the village of Burkittsville. The early afternoon sun had got quite warm, and Colonel Bartlett was sweating by the time he reached the Shafer farm. What he saw when he arrived surprised him. Lounging about in various degrees of repose after lunch, under some large shade trees in the Shafer's front yard were Generals Franklin, Slocum, Smith, Hancock, Brooks, and Newton, smoking cigars. All of them, West Point graduates and old friends, were debating the best plan of attack to drive the Confederates back up and over South Mountain. Colonel Bartlett was surprised again when suddenly General Slocum turned to him and asked him which route would he advise to attack the enemy, the one on the left or the one on the right? With his conversation with the local townsmen

Richard Krause still fresh in his mind, the Colonel immediately responded, "On the right."

"Well, gentlemen, that settles it," said General Franklin.

"Settles what, General?" Colonel Bartlett exclaimed.

"The point of attack."

Colonel Bartlett, in addition to being well liked by his men, had also garnered the respect of men like General Franklin and General Slocum whom he had fought under during the recent Virginia Peninsula Campaign. But now turning a little red in the face, he took it as an affront that he would be asked his opinion on such a vital decision especially without being present to hear what the gathered group of older, experienced generals had had to say about it. General Slocum, quickly noticing Bartlett's rising ire, reassured him by explaining:

"Colonel Bartlett, understand that General Brooks has just returned from personally inspecting the ground on the left and given his views. As a group here we were equally divided, which is why we wanted your opinion since you've just come from personally inspecting the ground on the right. Your view is equally valued," said General Slocum.

At that point General Franklin interrupted the conversation.

"So, who's going to lead the battle?" he asked, addressing the group at large.

"Bartlett," immediately replied General Slocum. Then General Slocum also appointed the Colonel in charge of deciding the attack formation. This certainly put Bartlett in a curious position as here he was, a brigade commander, deciding both the point of attack and the formation of troops of the entire VI Corps.

Colonel Bartlett suggested to General Franklin that they organize the formation of the three brigades, in column of regiments deployed, two regiments front, at one hundred paces interval between lines (giving them six lines). The head of the column should be directed to a point that he indicated to General Franklin, at nearly right angles to the road that crossed the mountain, and in a direction to strike the highest point of the road reached at the crest, it being the shortest line. Furthermore, the Colonel would deploy the 27th N.Y. as skirmishers at the head of the column, and skirmish into the teeth of the enemy's line of battle, following with the head of the column at one hundred paces. He would not halt after giving the order forward until they reached the crest of the mountain if possible. General Franklin approved of these suggestions and based his written order upon them.

As soon as General Franklin finished writing the orders for battle, he handed them to Colonel Bartlett and told him to proceed to prepare the troops to storm Crampton's Pass. Then he ordered Battery A, First Maryland Artillery to the left rear of Burkittsville. Confederate Artillery composed of Captain Basil Manly's 1st North Carolina's six-gun battery and one gun each from the Richmond Fayette Artillery and Magruder's Light Artillery from up on South Mountain in Brownsville Pass immediately engaged the Marylanders on the south side of Burkittsville. As the cannons roared back and forth at each other, at approximately 12:30 P.M. General Franklin sent a message to General McClellan that showed his own lack of confidence in carrying out his orders to carry Crampton's Gap.

Franklin penned this short note to McClellan: "I think from appearances that we may have a heavy fight to get the pass."

Earlier that morning while the VI Corps was resting outside the village of Jefferson, unwisely waiting for Couch's Division to join them, Franklin took an opportunity to pen a rushed letter to his wife Anna.

He wrote, "We start out from here this morning for Burkittsville and will I think have a battle before the day is over. If we are successful in getting over the Blue Ridge (South Mountain) we will doubtless find the enemy there and have other fights." Then alluding to earlier battles, First Bull Run, Fair Oaks and Savage's Station, he continued, "Is it not singular that everything seems to be done on Sunday?"

Then General Franklin did something that shocked everyone. Extinguishing his cigar, Franklin turned to the still assembled group of generals and said, "Men, come with me."

Walking down the country lane about a mile farther into town along Main Street, which was shielded by the buildings and houses from the enemy's artillery fire, the group of Union officers came to the entrance of a small, one-room church. The hot September sun was piercing the stained glass windows and lit up the single white spire that adorned the roof of the Resurrected Reformed Church. Removing their caps, they followed General Franklin through the large oak double doors and walked down the center aisle of old hand-carved pews and were met by the minister who appeared from behind the pulpit.

"Good afternoon, gentlemen," said Minister Long, greeting the group of uniformed officers. "I am Minister James Long, and this is our house of worship here in Burkittsville. What can I do for you on this lovely Sabbath?"

"Good afternoon, Minister Long. It's a pleasure to meet you. I'm General William B. Franklin, commander of the Union Army's VI Corps. Please pardon the disturbance going on to the west of your handsome village here. Had we had any choice, we would certainly have not chosen your village here or any of the towns and villages in Maryland to face the Confederates in battle. But, alas, we must fight the enemy where we meet them, and unfortunately today that is here, Minister Long," said General Franklin. "We would also have not chosen to fight them on Sunday when we would rather be worshipping our Lord. I assure you, Minister Long, we will do everything in our power to push the enemy up and over South Mountain to the west of your village and hope to thereby spare it from any further harm and shelling from enemy artillery. But before we continue this battle, I wonder if you would be so kind as to say a prayer for these fine officers and their soldiers who are about to do battle for this great United States of America?" asked the General.

"Why, why, of course General Franklin," replied Minister Long. "I'm deeply honored to serve my country and can't think of a better way to use my convocation to serve our Lord as well. Please, gentlemen, be seated in the front pews here and kneel down in prayer."

Minister Long, still wearing the vestments from this morning's service, lit the three candles directly in front and slightly below the pulpit. Red light poured through the stained glass windows illuminating a large crucifix hung on the back wall behind the pulpit of the old country church.

When the officers were all knelt in prayer, Minister Long began, "Our Father, who art in heaven, we beseech ye today to keep these soldiers safe from harm, these men who have come here to fight to protect this great country we live in; These men who have sworn to give their lives as necessary to keep this great nation, one nation, indivisible, under God. Go with them, oh Lord, give them the strength to carry on with their mission. Shield them from danger and safeguard them from Evil, so that one day all men will be free and equal, not only in the eyes of the Lord but in the eyes of all men. In Jesus' name we pray, Amen."

A round of Amens were heard from the generals in the front pew. As General Franklin rose to stand, General Slocum, rising to his feet as well, noticed a tear fall from Franklin's eye.

"Thank you, Minister Long. Thank you very much," said General Franklin. "My men and I are deeply grateful for your prayers. Now we must be going."

"Come men, let's get back to headquarters and see how Bartlett's been making out getting the troops ready," said General Franklin.

By the time the group of officers returned to Shafer's Farm, the sun had dropped considerably, and now was only just shining over the top of South Mountain. From the front yard of Martin Shafer's farm, Franklin used his hand to shield his eyes and looked westward over the top of South Mountain, noticing that the sun would recede behind the mountain soon. Every other officer's set of eyes followed General Franklin's.

CHAPTER VII

As Colonel Bartlett began to organize the troops of the VI Corps, he and his men also noticed the generals departing the Shafer farm, walking into the village of Burkittsville. Scratching his head in wonderment, the colonel was in disbelief. Where could they be going now? It was beginning to look to him like General Franklin did not wish to fight this battle today. What with the useless delay for a few hours this morning waiting for Couch outside Jefferson, and then the break while the men cooked their noon rations for lunch, the after lunch smoke break, and now what? Bartlett was very aware that they were wasting precious daylight.

But Colonel Bartlett was a good soldier, and he quickly dismissed the matter as none of his business. Getting down to the more pressing matters at hand, he proceeded to carry out Franklin's written orders as they had discussed. By the time General Franklin and the other officers returned, Bartlett had VI Corps prepared for battle, although by now they had been standing in the hot September sun for some time. Earlier, at approximately 2:00 P.M., a reply to Franklin's message to General McClellan had arrived and it was handed to Franklin as soon as he returned from the church. McClellan was near Boonsboro marshalling the remaining two thirds of his Union forces fighting two other separate battles approximately ten miles north on South Mountain, at Fox's and Turner's Gaps. His orders instructed Franklin to amass his troops and "carry Burkittsville at any cost." But McClellan's message also came with a qualifier that provided General Franklin with a little wiggle room. General McClellan's message went on to say:

"If you find the enemy in very great force at the pass, let me know at once, and amuse them as best you can so as to retain them there. In that event I probably will throw the mass of the Army on the pass in front of here. If I carry that it will clear the way for

you, and you must then follow the enemy as rapidly as possible." 2

2 quoted from *First to Last: The Life of Major William B. Franklin, by Mark A. Snell,* Pg 180

Once General McClellan had become in possession of Lee's Special Orders Number 191 and he had divided his Army of Potomac into the three wings to oppose him and attack him in the passes of South Mountain, he knew that for his plan to be carried out it was imperative that the mission assigned to his left wing under the command of General Franklin be successful. Despite McClellan's repeated warnings to General Halleck the Secretary of War back in Washington, that once Lee's Army of Virginia had crossed the Potomac, that they abandon the garrison in Harpers Ferry under the command of Colonel Dixon S. Miles, Halleck persisted. He ordered Colonel Miles to hold Harpers Ferry, whatever the cost.

McClellan insisted that due to the geography surrounding Harpers Ferry, it lying at the base of three mountains and on the banks of where the Shenandoah and Potomac Rivers meet, that it was indefensible now that the Confederates had crossed over the Potomac into Maryland. Fourteen thousand Federal troops occupied the garrison in Harpers Ferry and whatever McClellan thought of his boss' opinion, he was duty-bound to try and protect those forces still remaining there. If General Franklin VI Corps could make all speed to cross South Mountain at Crampton's Gap and attack Confederate forces led by General Lafayette McLaws' rear near Elk Ridge at the base of Maryland Heights, then perhaps Colonel Miles could hold off until more Federal reinforcements could come to his aid.

CHAPTER VIII

Rebecca Anne Burgard was far from being what might be considered a normal young woman of twenty years of age. But she had learned that when dancing with men like Captain Dunning, not to play up her tomboy character too much, or else it was back to being the dance wallflower. The truth of the matter went far beyond her bobbed red hair. Not only could Rebecca outshoot, outfish, and outhunt both of her brothers, one a year older and the other a year younger, she could also outride and outwrestle them. No matter how much her father and mother had tried to tame these qualities, sending her for dance and piano lessons and urging her to embrace her feminine side, Rebecca still wasn't happy unless she was roaming the woods hunting rabbits, squirrels, deer and anything else that might put food on the table. She knew every inch of South Mountain and the surrounding fields of Pleasant Valley better than most of the woodsmen that had grown up there.

Ever since her family had visited their relatives in Georgia, a change had come over her. When she wasn't out squirrel hunting in the tall pines of her uncle's plantation or wrestling her boy cousins to show off, Rebecca was sitting quietly in the parlor or on the veranda listening to all the talk of the impending War Between the States. It seemed like there was nothing else anyone was talking about. Uncle Bo had formed a militia and had begun organizing the local men and boys gathering on Saturday mornings to drill and march around the town square. Rebecca had begged her uncle to let her join too, but he just let out a hearty laugh and said, "What would all your Yankee friends up north think? A respectable young lady like yourself down here marching with a bunch of Rebels." He pinched her rosy cheek.

"Now you get along back in the kitchen and help your Aunt Thelma with the biscuits, or I'll have to tell your father about that wild boar you shot the other day."

Uncle Bo slapped his knee, laughed some more, and said, "If that didn't take all the dickens, a young filly like you staring down a 400-pound wild boar charging right at you and you just standing there until you could set your sights right between its eyes and dropping it right at your feet. You're damn lucky to be still standing here, Rebecca. Now git!"

When Rebecca entered the kitchen, her Aunt Thelma couldn't help notice the dried tears on her cheek.

"My Lord, what's the matter child? Have you been crying?" asked Thelma.

"Oh, it's nothing, Aunt Thelma. It's silly really. I just asked Uncle Bo if I could join his militia and he laughed at me. I know women aren't supposed to be able to go fight wars, but I can shoot a rifle better than most of those boys out there, and I want to help fight the Yankees too. I'll just have to find other ways to help the cause." Taking up a washcloth from the sink, Rebecca wiped her face and gave her aunt a big grin. "Now, let's get to baking those biscuits Uncle Bo was talking about. Those boys are going to be real hungry after all that marching and drilling this morning."

When Rebecca returned to Maryland with her family, she didn't forget about her uncles and cousins down south. She turned her eyes to every morsel and scrap of information about the war she could find. Every newspaper article, every notice posted at the bank or the post office, every story told by the old men that gathered on the porch of the Brownsville Store became part of her world and consumed her. She made a point to personally check for the mail every day at the post office, which was also located in the Brownsville Store. As soon as a letter arrived from her relatives, she would beg her father and mother to let her read it as soon as they had finished. When one of the letters brought the news that her cousin George had been killed, Rebecca wept bitterly. She made up her mind right then and there that if the war ever came to Pleasant Valley she would do whatever she could to help the Southern cause. She had long talks with Miss Bessie, her nanny, about freeing the slaves, and Miss Bessie always said that most of those negroes might want to think about how good they had it; and they might be sorry someday if they didn't have masters to take care of them anymore. Rebecca had secretly sewn herself a Confederate private's uniform and kept it folded and hidden under her mattress for when the day might come when she would need it.

When she returned home after the dance, she put on her nightgown and lifted up the mattress to make sure her uniform was still there. Then before drifting off to sleep, she remembered how that wicked Julia Brown had cut in on her one and only dance of the evening, and those captivating blue eyes of Captain Dunning looking back into her own.

CHAPTER IX

At approximately 2:30 P.M., Colonel Bartlett deployed his and General Slocum's former regiment, the 27th N.Y. as skirmishers, intending to skirmish into the teeth of their line of battle.

The 5th Maine led by Colonel Jackson and the 16th N.Y. under the command of Lt. Colonel Seaver followed. The 121st N.Y was held in reserve to guard prisoners under the command of Colonel Richard Franchot. Colonel Cake's 96th Pennsylvania, Bartlett's remaining regiment who had been spread out amongst the buildings of Burkittsville in skirmish formation were ordered to fall in behind. Hidden from the batteries they moved along a ravine to a stonewall bordering the "Forest" about 250 yards from the Confederate Line. Behind Bartlett's brigade, Brigadier General John Newton employed his command setting up two lines as well: the first line comprised of the 18th N.Y on the left and the 32nd N.Y. on the right. Newton's second line, the 31st N.Y. was

positioned on the left and the 95th Pennsylvania was on the right. Following in the similar formation of two lines were the New Jersey troops led by Colonel Alfred Torbert. The 2nd N.J. was on the left and the 1st N.J. on the right of the first line, and the 4th N.J and 3rd N.J. filling in the second line, left to right respectively.
3

3 (Unholy Sabbath: The Battle of South Mountain, by Brian Matthew Jordan, pg 266)

Tommy Krause was crouched on the floor of the cupola on the roof of Saint Paul's Lutheran Church next door to his family home on Main Street in Burkittsville. Only the very top of his head and his grandfather's naval spyglass protruded over the edge of the banister. From this perch Tommy had a birds-eye view of the entire battle that was about to ensue before him. It was not without some degree of danger for Tommy to be up there as the Rebels' artillery was lobbing shells in the general direction of the town and bullets were occasionally whizzing by. If Tommy's folks knew where he was, there would certainly be hell to pay. For almost an hour Tommy had been watching the Union troops amass their lines in front of him preparing for the fight. Now through the ancient spyglass Tommy saw the Confederate troops fortifying their positions along Mountain Church Road. As he focused the lens up and down the Confederate line, he observed cavalry troops dismounting their horses at both ends of the line. But then abruptly Tommy halted the glass near the end of the Confederate's left flank. The last soldier at the end of the line had just dismounted a stunning reddish mare with a white marking on its face shaped like a crescent moon. Tommy stared in disbelief. He crouched a little higher up above the railing so as to steady the glass better and twisted it to dial the focus in closer on the mare's face. Now he was absolutely certain. Everyone in Pleasant Valley knew that horse. Its name was Crescent and it belonged to Rebecca Burgard. She had won every steeple chase and fence jumping contest from Frederick to Hagerstown in the last three years riding Crescent, ever since she had brought it back from her family's plantation in Georgia. It had been a present to her from her Uncle Bo for her sixteenth birthday. But the question was what was it doing here on the front lines of the Confederate cavalry? Tommy squirmed to find a better position so as to try and focus the spyglass on the soldier's face that had just dismounted Crescent.

Blam! A bullet struck the banister, splintering the wood next to Tommy's hand and driving a sharp piece of wood into his knuckle. He ducked back down, almost dropping the spyglass over the side of the cupola. Blood poured from the wound on his hand as he removed the splinter and used his shirttail to wrap it to curtail the bleeding.

Tommy espies the battle from the church cupola.

Cavalryman Colonel Thomas Munford was the ranking Confederate commander at Crampton's Gap and he was becoming somewhat unnerved as he watched the large number of Bluecoats amass across his front. Just that morning Colonel William A. Parham's three regiments of Virginia infantry had arrived, which all told only amounted to roughly five hundred and fifty men. Colonel Munford didn't have a lot of options other than to position the Virginians to take the best advantage of the terrain before them, which fortunately provided some stone walls and picket fences that the Rebs could hide behind. Munford placed the 16th Virginia kneeling behind a stone wall on the right side, the 12th Virginia to the left of them, north of Burkittsville Road, and then the 6th Virginia filled out a very thin line of infantry to the left of them. Munford had his own 2nd Virginia Cavalry dismount and bolster the weak flanks on the right and the 12th Virginia Cavalry on the left.

Although Confederate Brigadier General Paul Semmes still kept the lions share of his brigade in

Brownsville Pass about a mile south of the ensuing battle at Crampton's Gap, on the morning of September 14th, he had become aware of General Jeb Stuart's demand that Crampton's Gap be held *"at all hazards."* Semmes therefore dispatched Colonel Edgar B. Montague's 32nd Virginia Infantry, a narrow picket line of two hundred men, to the base of the mountain joining Parham's Virginians. He also ordered his own 10th Georgia led by Major Willis Holt to Crampton's Gap. Holt had only just been given Colonel Parham's instructions for deployment when Semmes ordered the breathless Georgians to countermarch back to their original positions down on the Weverton-Rohrersville Road. Again Semmes was convinced that the battle shaping up at the base of Crampton's Pass was only a feint, and that soon the Union forces would turn in his direction towards Brownsville. Colonel Parham, *"seeing a large force of the enemy in line of battle approaching,"* scoffed at what he believed was an unreasonable decision and gave Major Holt preemptory orders *"to remain and to meet the emergency at hand."*

All told now, with the added Virginians and Georgians, the Confederate line established to prevent the Union forces from crossing South Mountain and spilling on over into Pleasant Valley, a short distance of about five miles from Harpers Ferry, was only some twelve hundred men, facing the Union's entire VI Corps, a daunting force that roughly outnumbered them ten to one.

The Confederates had *"strict orders"* to hold their fire until the enemy was *"within good rifle range."* No sooner than the last of the federal forces had been deployed as Colonel Bartlett had instructed, the assembled Confederate line *"briskly engaged"* them. *"The New Yorkers in the front dodged a hail of musketry fire and artillery from the heights above, and stopped to take refuge behind a split rail fence about two or three hundred yards away from the enemy."* General Slocum and his fellow officers, fully expecting an enemy infantry attack, had left all of their artillery in the rear. But now seeing that the enemy had taken cover behind a stone wall and worrying that the wall might prove to be an insurmountable obstacle to the advance of his lines, he began to make every effort to bring forward a battery of artillery in hopes of driving them from their position. It was obvious to Slocum now that the enemy, even if they were outnumbered, were in position to take the most advantage of their surroundings, being entrenched behind the stone wall and being higher up on the mountain firing down on the federal forces. For the first 10 or 15 minutes after General Slocum had given the order to advance Bartlett's first line, the 5th Maine and 16th New York hesitated. *"Finally, a great cheering, as if some welcome reinforcements swelled along the line, and over the fence they clambered,"* and started marching towards the Confederate line at *"double quick time."*

For the next three quarters of an hour Bartlett's regiments kept up a brisk fire. The lethal back and forth of musket fire *"left a line of killed and wounded Bluecoats and rebuffed, if temporarily, the survivors* several yards." When "the men in the embattled regiments looked to the rear for reinforcements," they "were surprised by what they saw... or didn't see." A frustrated Colonel Bartlett later reported, "By some unexplained and unaccountable mistake, more than a thousand yards intervened between the head of the column of General Newton's brigade and my own line." Bartlett knew his men couldn't hold their position for very long without running out of ammunition, so he rode back and found Newton's Brigade and ordered them up as replacements. Without support, the men from New York and Maine sustained the battle with "nothing but the most undaunted courage and steadiness." 4

4 quotes in italics are from *Unholy Sabbath, The Battle of South Mountain, Brian Mathew Jordan, pg's 267- 270*

CHAPTER X

Rebecca Burgard had hardly slept at all Saturday night. What with the excitement of the chicken supper and dance and the brief dance with Captain Dunning, not to mention that the Confederate 12th Virginia Cavalry were camped along the Weverton-Rohrersville Road practically in her own backyard, she tossed and turned. Finally when she heard the clock in the den strike five, she got out of bed. She lit a small candle and, while her brothers slept in their room down the hall, Rebecca reached under her mattress and pulled out the Confederate uniform she had sewn in secret. She took off her nightgown and pulled one of her brother's undershirts over her head. Then she put on the gray pants and shirt, some socks and her old riding boots, the ones she used for hunting, not her new ones she wore for shows. Reaching under the bed, she pulled out an old rucksack in which she had stowed away some biscuits with jam and a couple pieces of fried chicken wrapped in a towel she had saved from yesterday's supper. Using some of her brother's hair oil, she slicked back her red hair and combed it behind her ears. Donning the Confederate cap, she had made she took one last look at herself in the mirror. Not satisfied that she still looked too young, she made a mental note to remember to smear some mud on her face once she got out to the barn. Reaching into the bottom of her closet, she felt for the small canvas bag that held her pistol and bullets and powder. She stuffed it inside the rucksack, and taking up her rifle from the corner and the rolled up wool blanket from her bed, she slipped down the corridor towards the back door that led out to the barn. Under the cover of darkness and with little moonlight, she made it to the barn without any of the Rebels out in the yard seeing her. Other than the one soldier on guard who appeared to be occasionally dozing off, none of the rest of them was stirring. She grabbed a carrot out of the bag hanging inside the barn door and rubbed Crescent's mane as she quietly fed it to her. While her tawny reddish mare crunched the carrot,

Rebecca saddled her and tied her rucksack and blanket to the back of her saddle. Almost forgetting, she scooped a couple handfuls of oats into an old feed bag and tied it to the back of the saddle too. She led her horse by the reins out the backside of the barn, and they crossed the short clearing and disappeared into the woods. Hiding in the thick woods behind the barn, Rebecca was now only twenty yards away from the camped cavalrymen. Kneeling on the ground, she picked up a handful of dirt and spit in it and rubbed a little of the mud on her cheeks.

In the pre-dawn light Rebecca noticed another large group of cavalry ride into the Rebel camp from up the road. A small group of what appeared to be officers emerged from a tent to greet them. As the officer on the lead horse dismounted, Rebecca immediately recognized him from his long blond hair and beard. It could be no other than the famous cavalryman-- General J.E.B Stuart. Rebecca had seen plenty of pictures of Stuart in the paper and her heart paced rapidly now at seeing him in person.

She thought she needed to take deep breaths in order to keep from fainting. Then she reminded herself how silly she was being. If she intended to join up with these men and fight Yankees, she needed to get hold of herself. From her hiding place behind the trees and the brush, she couldn't quite make out what was being said. A few more minutes went by, and then General Stuart and the men he had rode in with quickly remounted and rode off down the road to the south towards Harpers Ferry. A minute after that, the orders to strike camp were issued and the tent that had previously housed the cavalry officers was struck. It seemed like in almost no time everyone was up and rolling up their blankets from where they had slept on the ground. Orders went out to fall in, and the men mounted their horses and lined up. As the first rays of sunlight pierced through the clouds, Rebecca mounted Crescent, and while all eyes were facing the road, she quietly rode the scant distance from the neighboring woods and joined the back of the line.

CHAPTER XI

Rebecca dismounted Crescent and loosely fastened her reins to a branch near where the other Rebel cavalrymen had tied their horses. She quickly spread a couple handfuls of oats on the ground before taking up her rifle and bag with the ammunition and then joining the others kneeling behind a split-rail fence at the end of the line on the far end of the left flank. She loaded her pistol and jammed it down in her belt. No sooner had she finished loading her rifle, she heard a great wailing sound of men and saw the army of Bluecoats running towards them. She too heard the whispers coming down the line to hold their fire until the enemy was in good firing range. Her rifle, although it packed a solid kick, was built for hunting deer and other game at long range. The hot, late afternoon sun was beating down on her shoulders, and a drop of sweat rolled off her nose as she squinted to take aim. Although the brunt of the Union infantrymen were charging for the center of the Confederate line, from Rebecca's position she could still draw a bead on some of the Bluecoats that were on the Union's right flank. As soon as the order to fire was given, Rebecca squeezed the trigger and a Union soldier fell to the ground.

Back in Burkittsville, Tommy Krause again peeped over the banister of the cupola, but all he could see now was a long line of musket smoke following the line of the base of South Mountain. Darn, he thought, now he'd probably never know why Crescent was being ridden by a Confederate cavalryman. Scratching his head with his good hand, he crouched back down in the cupola and wondered what he should do. He knew it was useless to try to get any closer to the battle; everyone had been given strict orders to stay put.

Rebecca kept loading her rifle and firing as quickly as she could. The long range of the deer rifle proved effective because she was able to make every shot count. Every bullet she fired, another soldier in blue hit the ground. A Confederate cavalryman eight feet away from her, crouching behind the fence, couldn't help but notice Rebecca and her long barreled rifle. Just as he looked her way and smiled a Union bullet struck him in the chest and he tumbled to the ground. Now her face was not only covered with sweat but also tears were streaming from her eyes. She scrambled over to the fallen Reb, but he was already dead. Remembering that she hadn't brought any water, she took the dead man's canteen and took a long drink. Despite the constant barrage of southern rifle fire and artillery, the Union infantrymen continued to advance. Where could they all possibly be coming from Rebecca wondered. It was as if McClellan's whole army was before them. Looking down the line of Confederates through the thick musket smoke, she saw that the center of the line had given way to the Bluecoats and the Rebels on both sides were retreating. Several cavalrymen of the 12th Virginia were now also retreating in her direction, so she joined them. They ran to their horses and mounted, falling back up the mountain behind a stone wall along Mountain Church road several hundred yards back. Here they quickly dismounted and joined the Georgians of the 10th regiment as they resumed firing down the mountain into the cheering, advancing Union infantrymen. Scrambling behind the wall with her rifle and ammunition, Rebecca suddenly found her self face to face with Captain Dunning. Recognizing her immediately, the handsome Captain was aghast.

"Lord, have mercy, child. What in the world are you doing here?"

"Killing Yankees. Same as you Captain. And from the looks of things," she said pointing down the mountain, "we better git to it." She loaded her rifle and took aim down the mountain, and another soldier in blue fell to the ground.

Still in shock, Captain Dunning whispered into Rebecca's ear, "This ain't no place for a woman," as he too took aim down the mountain.

"I reckon I've killed as many Yankees as the next man today," Rebecca replied as she reloaded, grinning at the Captain the whole time. "My uncle lives in Georgia and is a Colonel in the Confederate Army, and my cousin George was killed last year, so it's only fair I join in too, now that the war has come to me."

"I've seen it all now. Well since you're here, come with me. Follow me, men!"

Rebecca and the Georgians followed him to a position around the stone Tritt house and opened fire against the right side of the 96th Pennsylvania. Rebecca kept up a steady fire crouched beside Captain Dunning when a Union bullet struck the Captain in the knee. As the front was pressing heavily now, the luckless Georgians had no choice but to fall back from the protection of the wall and into the road, and then up the side of the mountain towards Whipp's Ravine. Two of Captain Dunning's infantrymen supported him on both sides and began to try to walk him up the road.

"Here, put him on my horse!" shouted Rebecca as they retreated up the mountain. The two infantrymen lifted the Captain into Crescent's saddle, and Rebecca leaped on in front. When they had reached an area behind some trees Rebecca dismounted and tore a piece off of the feed bag and tied it tightly around Captain Dunning's knee. She opened the canteen and trickled water down his throat until he seemed to be revived. The Confederates were running up the mountain in complete disorder as the men of the 3rd and 4th New Jersey sprung up with a cheer, and enthusiastically joined the front line.

Near Whipp's Ravine, Privates James Allen and James Richards of the Union's 16th New York had become separated from their unit. As they got closer to the base of the mountain, Private Richards was struck by a bullet in his left leg. Private Allen found a comfortable spot for Richards to rest at the trunk of a large oak tree and then continued to follow the retreating Confederates. The only thing left for Allen to do was to climb up the mountain too. As he drew himself up he was met with another volley and was slightly wounded. Private Allen put on a bold face, waved his arms, and yelled to his imaginary company: "Up men, up!" The Rebels of the 16th Georgia, thinking they were cornered, stacked their arms. Then Private Allen made haste to get between them and their guns and found he had captured fourteen prisoners and a flag from their color guard.

A short distance a little further to the south, the Union's 4th Vermont had pursued Munford's retreating Virginians from a stone wall near the foot of the mountain to an unused wagon track on the eastern slope of the mountain. Once there, First Lieutenant George W. Hooker led four companies south to attempt to silence the Confederate guns still firing from Brownsville Pass. Hooker, who had ridden ahead of his men, came upon a group of Confederate soldiers. Acting alone, he confronted 116 men of the 16th Virginia. He told them that a large Union force was near and convinced them to surrender.

CHAPTER XII

As the Confederate Infantrymen of the 10th Georgia and the Cavalrymen of the two regiments from Virginia continued to retreat up the eastern face of South Mountain, they were joined by Brigadier General Howell Cobb's Brigade of Infantrymen from Athens, Georgia who had just arrived. Earlier in the afternoon, around 1 P.M., Confederate General Lafayette McLaws had ordered General Cobb to countermarch from Sandy Hook to join up with General Semmes in Brownsville. For some unknown reason it took Cobb's Brigade three hours to march to Brownsville, a distance of only five miles. When Cobb arrived, he went into Semmes' camp but did not report immediately to General Semmes, thereby wasting another hour of precious time. When General Cobb received the orders from Thomas Munford to come up at once to Crampton's Gap, it finally registered to Howell Cobb that this was indeed an urgent matter. He immediately dispatched his two strongest regiments, the 24th Georgia and 15th North Carolina. But before the head of the column had stepped into the road, Cobb received another urgent message from Colonel Parham at the Gap that the enemy was pressing him hard with overwhelming numbers and appealed to him for all the support he could bring. Then General Cobb formed up his remaining two regiments, the 16th Georgia and the Cobb Legion, and accompanied them in person. This time they marched as quickly as possible, the General realizing the extreme emergency awaiting. By the time Cobb reached the battlefront, Crampton's Gap was already as good as lost.

Captain Dunning had also realized that there was no way the Confederates were going to be able to stop the sheer numbers of the enemy charging up South Mountain. Shielded behind some trees and bushes sitting on Rebecca's horse, Crescent, he knew he had to figure out a way to get this young woman out of here alive. He knew also that Rebecca would never just give up. The little he knew about her only having met her the day before, if she was anything, it was tenaciously stubborn when she had her mind made up. The Captain noticed a dead Union soldier lying on the ground about ten feet away. He had a plan.

"Rebecca, we're not going to win this battle today. There's just too many Yankees and not enough of us. Quickly, help me dismount for a minute. I've got an idea," said Captain Dunning.

Rebecca nervously helped him off her horse.

"Now, Rebecca, you want to help the Southern cause, don't you?"

"Yes, of course, I'm here killing Yankees, aren't I?"

"Well then, it's not going to do anybody any good if you go and get yourself killed in a battle we're going to lose anyway. So here's what I think we should do. Go back over there behind those bushes and take off your Confederate uniform. I'm going to take the blue uniform off this dead soldier here and hand it over to you. I want you to put it on and to pretend to be on the other side. I realize now I let myself be tricked last night by your friends, Julia

Brown and Tommy Krause. When they asked me to escort Tommy back to Burkittsville by way of Crampton's Gap, I let Tommy scout our position and now I'm sure that the information was given to the Union forces. Otherwise, how would they have known to attack Crampton's Gap, the one less guarded by our forces, and not take the southern route over Brownsville Pass where we were waiting for them?

"What's done is done, but you can help us make up for this mistake. Eventually, later this evening when they finish routing us and send us running back down into Pleasant Valley, General William B. Franklin, the man in charge of all these Union troops is going to come up to the top of Crampton's Gap to survey his position. You need to find a way to get close enough to him to persuade him to go back to his camp in Burkittsville tonight and to not press us first thing in the morning. Basically, we need you to help buy us some more time. Even an hour or two in the morning could make a huge difference. Will you do it? Please, I beg of you. I feel absolutely horrible that I let that pretty young Julia turn my head last night," pleaded Captain Dunning.

"Of course, of course, Captain Dunning, I'll do the best I can," stammered Rebecca as she slipped behind the bushes and began undressing. "But what about you, Captain? What's going to happen to you?"

"I'll be fine, if I can just borrow your horse for a few more hours, since I can't walk on this busted knee. I'll leave her back at your barn once we retreat back into Pleasant Valley. Once I join back up with my men, they'll help get me to a field hospital. I think they're setting up a temporary hospital in that church, the one called St. Luke's up on the hill as you head south out of Brownsville," said the Captain.

The whole Confederate line was under fire, and the pressure asserted by the Union forces forced them running up the hillside pell-mell in retreat. Colonel Bartlett flashed a smile to his fellow Union soldiers as he noticed the line of musket smoke steadily moving up the mountain, a sure sign that they were gaining ground and would eventually carry the day. When Confederate General Cobb arrived, a weary Thomas Munford explained the position of the troops and attempted to turn over to him the command. Despite his seniority, Cobb refused to take on the responsibility. At the General's request, Munford personally positioned the 24th Georgia and 15th North Carolina, deploying them on the left. Colonel Munford then directed Cobb to take his smaller regiments down the Gapland Road to support the badly beaten up flank on the right. Lieutenant Colonel Jefferson Lamar, in charge of the Cobb Legion and the 16th Georgia led by Lieutenant Colonel Philip Thomas, started down the wooded slope above Mountain Church Road. Thomas' regiment was on the left and Lamar's on the right. Colonel Munford tried to bring the troops into line but before doing so the most awful commotion began. Wounded men heading for the rear were passing through the makeshift line, increasing the confusion and thereby contributing to the growing overall sense of despair and defeat. Colonel Munford saw General Cobb attempting to rally the men, but it was useless. Munford remembered thinking he may as well have been trying to rally a flock of frightened sheep.

The 96th Pennsylvania and New Yorkers from the 32nd and 18th regiments had continued pressing up the mountainside near Whipp's Ravine towards the Confederate left flank. By now they had rolled over the 10th Georgia and soon Cobb's 24th Georgia turned and also fled back up the hill. The 15th North Carolina did the same. On the left side of the Union line Colonel Alfred Torbert's New Jersey troops, numbering twelve hundred men and bolstered by their rout of the Virginians, sited enemy troops ahead and to their right and marched directly for them. This was Lt. Colonel Jefferson Lamar's ill-fated Cobb's Legion, a force of only two hundred-fifty men. Lamar had to decide to turn and run back up the mountain or to stand and fight to give the others a chance to escape. Lamar chose to fight. In the fervor of the battle, some of Lamar's Georgians madly leapt the stone wall in front of them, the only remaining protection from the enemy fire, and rushed the advance columns of the Bluecoats from New Jersey. It only hastened their deaths. Under ever more pressing fire from the men from New Jersey, the Georgians of Cobb's Legion became pinned down. The 3rd New Jersey regiment had worked their way around to the right of and behind them and had begun to force the Georgians to fight the enemy on two sides. Men from the Legion began to break and scramble up the steep hillside despite Lamar pleading for them to stand and fight. Soon after, Lamar fell to the ground when a bullet smashed into his leg. Finally, he ordered a retreat by his left flank, but before he himself could get away, he was shot in the chest and mortally wounded. Approximately eighty per cent of Cobb's Legion were either killed or captured.

CHAPTER XIII

Towards evening Lieutenant Henry Jennings had settled into his bivouac at the base of Maryland Heights when orders arrived instructing them to make all speed for Crampton's Gap. Jennings was assigned to the Troup Light Artillery, under Cobb's Legion, a battery of two ten-pounder Parrot rifles and two smoothbore bronze howitzers, a twelve-pounder called the "Jennie" and a six-pounder named the "Sallie Craig." The two long-range, rifled Parrot guns had been laboriously carried up to Maryland Heights above Harpers Ferry, but the two shorter-range bronze guns, commanded by Jennings, had remained at the foot of the mountain. At the very top of Crampton's Gap at the intersection of Gapland Road and Arnoldstown Road was an open field that belonged to George W. Padgett. On the east a wooden, rail fence lined the road and a low stone wall bordered the field to the west. Here General Howell Cobb, with the other commanders, Colonel Tom Munford and Colonel

Parham, tried their best to rally their beaten troops for a last-ditch defense. While the remains of the 10th, 16th, and 24th Georgia regiments gathered, suddenly the New Jersey troops charged up the road from the southeast and hurled a deadly volley on the 24th's right flank. General Semmes joined General Cobb on the field and even though at extreme exposure, with great coolness, he gave his cordial aid and cooperation. All of Cobb's staff was on the field and helped do all that could be done under the circumstances. One of Cobb's staff, who had been standing next to the General, was his aide-de-camp and also his brother-in-law, Colonel John Basil Lamar. A bullet struck Lamar in the chest. Cobb carried him, dying, off the field. The Georgians broke under the pressure. General Cobb took their colors and ordered them to take a stand. Some of them ignored him and continued their flight while others formed behind the wall to wait for the Federals. They didn't have to wait long. When the head of the Union column rounded the corner and headed towards the Gap, they were engaged by fire of the Confederate muskets and the two guns of the Troup Light Artillery. After a brisk march from Sandy Hook, Lt. Henry Jennings with "Jennie" and "Sallie Craig" had just arrived on the field, and the blast caught the men from New Jersey off guard. The column of Bluecoats shrank back but only briefly. The New Jersey Brigade's blood was up, and they were not to be denied. As the Federal tide moved continually forward, the New Jersey troops had again turned the right flank of the Georgian's line. Resistance collapsed and the rest of the Confederate troops joined their compatriots in headlong retreat into Pleasant Valley below.

Edgar Richardson was working the gun crew of the "Sallie Craig," and they had come up at the double quick, in what was now nearly pitch dark. As they reached the summit of the Gap, they met some of Cobb's men already running for their lives. Cobb was still trying to rally his men, and as they passed him, General Cobb hollered, "here is the Troup Artillery men, rally to it!" but only one man came back. By this time the Federals were less than a hundred yards away, and Richardson lobbed five rounds, hoping to hold them back. He fired right into the head of their column and cut down their colors, thinking he must have killed at least a few of them. The "Jennie" wasn't as lucky. It only managed to shoot off three rounds before the Union muskets tore apart her axle, rendering her useless. The artillerists feared losing "Sallie Craig," so they limbered her and fled back down Gapland Road from which they'd just came up a few minutes ago, leaving "Jennie" behind. 5

5 *Unholy Sabbath, The Battle of South Mountain, by Brian Matthew Jordan, pg 283*

Colonel Bartlett was highly impressed with the enemy artillery's great skill and bravery.

"Their infantry had ceased firing and was nowhere in sight, but as I emerged from the woods I saw the flash of a cannon, which was within fifty yards of me and trained toward us, the canister bursting in our

very faces. It was limbered to the rear in an instant, and at twenty paces had passed the other gun of the section, which delivered its fire, limbered up, and went scurrying down the road before any but a scattering fire could be brought against it." 6

6 quoted from Park Service sign posted in the battlefield at Crampton's Gap

CHAPTER XIV

Brigadier General William B. Franklin chuckled to himself as he watched the line of musket smoke slowly progress up the side of South Mountain. He was pleased, albeit a little surprised, that the battle had gone so well for his Federal forces. "Bye jove, Bartlett and Slocum and the rest of the men had pulled it off quite smartly," he thought. He ordered a detail of officers and men on horseback, followed by a small regiment of Infantrymen, to join him on Gapland Road where they proceeded to file up the mountain. A considerable distance separated his party and those on up ahead still fighting the enemy. About halfway up the mountain, they paused to listen to the cannon fire coming from the top.

Rebecca bit her lip as she watched Captain Dunning ride Crescent up the mountain and disappear from her sight. Looking down at herself, wearing the blue Union uniform with the bloody tear in the shirt from a bullet hole, she shuddered in fear for an instant. Cautiously she emerged from the bushes and looked about for other Federal troops. She could hear raging gunfire and see the musket smoke coming from a patch of woods up to her right and farther up the mountain. The last thing she wanted to happen now that she had come this far was to be shot by a southerner and be found dead on the battlefield wearing a Yankee uniform. Yet it also wouldn't be good to be caught walking back down the mountain in the direction of Burkittsville and be discovered and charged as a deserter. After carefully thinking this through, she realized that the best thing she could do was to position herself where she would have a good view of anyone coming up Gapland Road and wait for General Franklin to come to her. At least it was getting later and soon it would be dark. Somehow that was a comfort to her unsettled mind. From her vantage point she could look down Gapland Road and see anyone who might round the bend coming in her direction.

Just then a group of Federal Cavalrymen rounded the corner. Rebecca slipped back behind the bushes to watch them. The group of soldiers in the front had their pistols drawn. As they approached, Rebecca noticed the officer riding a few paces back was wearing the uniform of a Union General; she recognized it from the pictures of General McClellan she had seen in the newspaper. That had to be General Franklin, she thought, and she took careful notice of his face and his long dark mustaches and dark beard as he rode by. When the last of the Infantrymen had passed her, she stepped out of the woods and fell in line at the rear.

General Franklin looked up Gapland Road and could see the reflection of the orange cannon fire in the distance at the top of Crampton's Gap. But then the loud cannon fire stopped and loud cheering could be heard echoing down the mountain.

"Well, men, sounds like we've beaten them!" exclaimed General Franklin.

Franklin's procession continued up Gapland Road. When they reached the top, they joined Colonel Bartlett and the others celebrating their hard-fought victory. Rebecca quietly moved up closer to the circle of officers who were lighting cigars and patting each other on the back, boasting of their smart and finally decisive win over their southern enemies. General Franklin, still mounted on his horse, lit a cigar and smiled proudly at his officers, especially to Colonel Bartlett.

A rabbit bolted from some nearby underbrush and ran directly under the front legs of General Franklin's horse. His horse spooked and reared back on its hind legs, throwing the General to the ground. He threw out his arm to cushion the fall, but his head landed on a rock and he was knocked out cold. Immediately a group of officers surrounded the fallen General. Rebecca forced her way into the circle.

"Please let me through!" shouted Rebecca in the lowest, manliest voice she could muster, "I studied

A rabbit spooks General Franklin's horse.

medicine in school," she said. The group of officers stood back to let her through.

"Does anyone have a canteen of water?" she asked as she pulled her handkerchief from her pocket. Someone passed her a canteen, and she wet the handkerchief and daubed General Franklin's forehead with it. As she checked his pulse, she asked for something soft to place under his head. The men gently lifted his head and placed a rolled up blanket under it.

A few minutes passed and the General came to. He was groggy and as his vision focused, he tried to stand on his feet. Rebecca held the wet handkerchief to his forehead and keeping him from standing, said: "Be still and rest for a moment, General Franklin. You've just taken a nasty fall and you've got a big bump and a small cut on your head. Your pulse is erratic and you're going to need to get in bed and lie still for a while. I think you may have a mild concussion."

"Who are you?" asked General Slocum.

"I'm just a private, sir," replied Rebecca, "but I studied medicine in Baltimore before enlisting."

"I think he's right, General Franklin," piped up General Slocum, "we'll have the men set up a small camp up here for the night and get you back to Mr. Shafer's farm where you can get a good night's rest and have a doctor look in on you first thing in the morning. You men there, help the General to his feet when he's ready and help him get back on his horse. Private, uh, pointing at Rebecca, I want you to stay close to General Franklin until he gets safely back to the Shafer farm. And thank you for your quick action in coming to his aid."

"Yes sir, you're welcome, sir," replied Rebecca, saluting the General.

CHAPTER XV

Tommy Krause had also watched the line of musket smoke move steadily up the mountain as twilight approached. In moments when the smoke cleared, he caught the last of the sunlight gleaming on the bayonets as the two enemy forces clashed. When the cannon fire had seemed to stop at the top of South Mountain, he crawled back down from the cupola and walked next door and stepped through his back door into his kitchen. He poured a pitcher of water from the buckets under the sink and washed and bandaged his hand from where he had been injured from the banister splinter. He was heading back to his bedroom when he heard his father's voice calling him.

"Tommy, Tommy, come on and help with harnessing up the horses to the farm wagon," he heard his father shout from the kitchen. Tommy came back down the stairs and joined his father.

"What are we harnessing up the wagon for?" Tommy asked. "It's dark outside."

"Fill up a couple of lanterns with oil too, Tommy, and bring the jug of lamp oil along. It's going to be a long night. The deacons from church are organizing rescue parties to go and pick up the wounded, and have asked for volunteers," replied Richard Krause. Mrs. Krause had already started tearing up old sheets into bandages and filling water jugs in the kitchen.

"Tommy, when you finish harnessing up the team, fill up these water buckets again at the spring too. Those men that have been fighting all day are now lying out there dying, some of them of thirst," said Mr. Krause as he started carrying water jugs out to the barn to load into the wagon.

Teams of farm wagons were lining up on Main Street in Burkittsville. Makeshift ambulances formed up, manned by the local citizens not knowing what horrors they were about to encounter on the hillsides of South Mountain. When Tommy finished harnessing the horses and loading the buckets of water and lanterns into the wagon, he ran next door to his neighbor and best friend's house, Jeff Higgins.

Tommy knocked on the door and Jeff opened it. Tommy and Jeff had been best friends since they were little boys, ever since the Higgins had moved into the house next door to the Krause's. They fished, hunted, worked in the fields and did everything together. They were like shadows of each other, and you almost never saw the one without the other being right behind him.

"Come on, Jeff, tell your folks you're coming with father and me to go pick up the wounded on South Mountain," said Tommy. "It's bound to be a long night, so bring some of your mother's jelly biscuits too."

Mr. Krause, Tommy, and Jeff swung the farm wagon on to Main Street and joined the line of wagons heading west towards the base of South Mountain. In the dim lantern light, they could just barely make out a group of Union officers and soldiers coming in their direction down Main Street. The line of wagons halted to let the officers get by.

As they passed the Krause's wagon, Tommy stared at the group of Union soldiers. Tommy's jaw dropped when he realized that staring right back at him was a Union soldier that looked exactly like Rebecca Burgard. When she noticed that he recognized her, she quietly put her finger to her lips, signaling Tommy to not reveal her secret. The group of Union soldiers continued eastward through Burkittsville heading off in the direction of Martin Shafer's farm on the eastern side of town.

As Mr. Krause guided the wagon up the road, Tommy whispered to Jeff, "If that don't beat all, Jeff. I just saw Rebecca Burgard wearing a Union uniform back there in that detachment of Union officers and soldiers."

"Psaww! You're losing your marbles, Tommy. It couldn't have been," replied Jeff.

"I wouldn't have believed it myself, but when she saw that I recognized her, she put her finger to her lips to hush me," said Tommy. "I swear it was Rebecca. I could see her red hair under the Union cap. And you know how she always favored a tomboy. It was definitely her!"

"Wonder what in the world she's up to now? Those Burgards are a little odd, but I wouldn't have expected any of them to be fighting on the Union side," said Jeff. "Didn't they move up here from somewhere down south, Georgia, or some place like that?"

Tommy leaned closer and whispered into Jeff's ear, "And I'll tell you something else that's even more odd. At the beginning of the battle, I was up in the cupola over at Saint Paul's Church with grandfather's old naval spyglass, and I would swear I saw Rebecca's red mare Crescent up there being dismounted by a Rebel soldier. You know the markings on her horse. You couldn't mistake that horse anywhere. Something's going on that's for sure."

Tommy and his friend Jeff soon forgot all about Rebecca Burgard and the mysteries surrounding her. The wounded men from both sides lay scattered up and down the mountainside, and shrieks and howls of pain and agony pressed upon their ears throughout the night. Gapland Road was crowded with both civilian and military ambulances, supply wagons, and groups of guarded Rebel soldiers all trying to get back to the rear in Burkittsville. Richard Krause and the two boys made countless trips up and down the dusty road, ferrying the wounded back to town where temporary hospitals had been set up in the town's two churches. The carpet in the Reformed Resurrection Church became so stained and soaked with blood they had to tear it up and remove it, and a pile of bloody amputated arms and legs grew outside the window where the surgeons had been busy operating all night.

CHAPTER XVI

For the first time in Rebecca Burgard's life, she was truly afraid. Staring down a charging wild boar in Georgia and getting shot at by Yankees hadn't fazed her in the least, but now she was effectively a spy in the Union ranks. Beads of nervous perspiration had formed on her upper lip. As she rode through Burkittsville with the small group of soldiers attached to General Franklin's party, she tried to formulate a plan to carry out her mission to detain the Union forces in the morning. Fortunately, Rebecca had gone to school with Sarah Shafer, and even though she had for the most part been a loner in school, she and Sarah had become friends, mainly for the reason that Sarah too was somewhat of a tomboy. She had grown up on her parent's farm and had milked the cows and fed the chickens and learned to ride and shoot just like Rebecca had.

When the General's party arrived back at camp, Rebecca helped General Franklin get onto his cot and lie down. Then she excused herself to go fetch some fresh cold water and some clean rags to bandage the General's head and to seek out Dr. Garrott. She walked up on the Shafer's back porch and knocked on the kitchen door.

Sarah Shafer opened the door and asked, "How can I help you, sir?"

Rebecca whispered, "Sarah it's me, Rebecca," and entered the kitchen.

"Why, Rebecca, you scared the death out of me! What are you doing wearing a Yankee uniform? You look just like a Yankee soldier," said Sarah.

"Shhh," replied Rebecca. "I don't have time to explain right now. Get me some clean rags and a pitcher of cold water for General Franklin. His horse got spooked up on Crampton's Gap and he's got a big bump and a cut on his head."

Sarah came back with the rags and poured a pitcher of spring water out of one of the buckets near the sink.

"Thanks, Sarah. Now I'm going to run back over to the General's tent and bandage his head. Go over to Dr. Garrott's and ask him to come and check on

General Franklin. He's in the first big tent over there with the lantern hanging just outside," said Rebecca, pointing out the kitchen door. "If Dr. Garrott's not at home, he's probably over at one of the churches where they've set up field hospitals. Tell him it's important. General Franklin's fallen off his horse and probably has a concussion. Later, I'll be back and I'll need to borrow a dress from you, so I can get out of this uniform and try and get back home."

"All right, Miss Rebecca Burgard. I'll do as you ask, but tomorrow you're going to have a lot of explaining to do," said Sarah.

Rebecca returned to the General's tent and helped him sit up and drink some water. She poured some water on a clean rag and wiped the dried blood from the cut on his forehead.

General Franklin drank most of the water down and then spit the rest out on the ground. "Confound it, soldier! That's enough water to drown me. Reach under my cot there and fetch my brandy!"

Rebecca found the bottle of brandy, handed it to him, and then told him she was going to check on the doctor. A few minutes later, Dr. Garrott arrived and Rebecca greeted him outside General Franklin's tent. She told him about the accident, how it had happened, and how she had treated him so far. She explained that she had taken some medical classes in Baltimore, where her cousin had studied for a time, and that General Slocum had entrusted her with General Franklin's care. It was her opinion that the General had suffered a mild concussion and if the doctor agreed perhaps he could administer a sedative so that he would rest comfortably for the night, and then he would probably feel better in the morning. Dr. Garrott examined the patient and concurred with Rebecca's diagnosis. He administered the sedative, apologized for his abrupt departure, explaining he had to get back to the field hospital because more and more wounded were arriving from the battlefield every minute.

Rebecca assured Dr. Garrott that there was no need for him to check on General Franklin in the morning, especially since it looked like the doctor had a long night ahead of him treating the wounded. As soon as the General was sleeping soundly, she excused herself from the soldiers attending to him, saying she had better get back and report to her unit. She went back to the Shafer farmhouse and threw a few small pebbles at Sarah's window. Sarah came to the window and saw Rebecca standing below. She went down to the kitchen door and let her in. It was almost midnight and Rebecca was dead on her feet. Not even bothering to take off her uniform, Rebecca curled up on one side of Sarah's bed.

"Whatever happens, don't let me sleep past sunup, Sarah. I have to count on you to make sure I wake up before dawn. Please, it's very important. Oh, and I need a dress. Just stuff it in my pack here and I'll take it with me in the morning," said Rebecca. As soon as she laid her head on the pillow she was fast asleep.

CHAPTER XVII

Both Sarah and Rebecca were awake before dawn on Monday morning, September 15th. By candlelight in Sarah's room, Rebecca whispered her account of herself and her activities for the last twenty-four hours. Sarah was aghast. Then Rebecca explained how she needed to find a way to detain General Franklin and his troops from rejoining the battle this morning. Although Sarah's parents were pro-Union Sarah had practically grew up as Rebecca's sister at Pleasant Hill and had secretly adopted Rebecca's views on the war.

"Sarah, didn't you tell me once that your mother had to take medicine for her headaches," whispered Rebecca.

"Yes, she keeps a bottle of laudanum in the cabinet in the kitchen," replied Sarah.

She went down to the kitchen and made a fire in the stove and brewed a pot of coffee. She got the bottle of laudanum from the cabinet and poured some in a cup of coffee. Just before sunup, Rebecca carried the cup of coffee to General Franklin's tent. The General was just waking up.

"Good morning, General Franklin," said Rebecca greeting the General.

"What's so good about it," grumbled back the General. "I feel like someone knocked me in the head last night."

"I'm not surprised you don't remember," replied Rebecca. "Your horse got spooked by a rabbit and threw you, and you landed on your head on a rock. You had a pretty big bump on your forehead and a small cut. Here. Take a sip of coffee and let me take this bandage off and have a look."

"Who the hell are you? Are you a doctor?" asked General Franklin.

"No sir, I'm just a private, but I attended medical classes in Baltimore before I enlisted, and I was there when you fell off your horse. General Slocum asked me to look after you," replied Rebecca.

"Well, hurry up and get me bandaged up. I need to get back to the front as soon as possible," said General Franklin as he finished his cup of coffee.

"Yes, sir. I'm just going to wash this cut out and put some salve on it and replace this dirty bandage with a fresh one and you'll be all set," said Rebecca.

By the time Rebecca finished wrapping the fresh bandage on the General's forehead, he slumped back down on his cot and fell fast asleep. She placed his blanket back over him and hid the coffee cup out of sight underneath his cot. The sun had come up and had begun to slowly climb up the eastern edge of South Mountain. Faintly off in the distance to the south cannon fire could be heard. When Rebecca stepped out of General Franklin's tent, she was greeted by General Slocum, General Baldy Smith, and a few other officers.

"Well, how's our patient this morning?" asked General Slocum.

"Good morning, sirs. He's still pretty groggy. He awoke for a few minutes while I cleaned out the wound and replaced the bandage with a fresh one. He didn't remember falling off his horse, so I reminded him of what had happened. Then he gave me strict orders to awaken him no later than seven when he said he would lead his men back to the top of Crampton's Gap to assess the battle plan for today," said Rebecca.

"That settles it then, men. No point in us all running off half-cocked without a good breakfast in our bellies," said General Slocum. "Get the cook fires going and fry up some bacon and eggs. Hell, these men deserve a good meal after the fight they had yesterday. Cut up some taters and fry them up too."

CHAPTER XVIII

Colonel Bartlett also woke before dawn on Monday, September 15th. It was so late when he laid down the night before, and he was so tired from the battle that he didn't bother to set up a tent. Instead he just spread his blankets right on the ground. Checking his watch, he realized there was still time to dispatch a messenger to General Franklin's headquarters back at the Shafer Farm. He was eager to get orders so that they might be able to capitalize on yesterday's win of taking Crampton's Gap and get an early start marching towards Harpers Ferry. With the messenger dispatched for orders, he built a fire and put on a pot of coffee. He tried to take his mind off yesterday's battle, but try as he might the vision of the battle the day before would just not go away. Scene after scene came rolling back in his mind, and as if in a dream, he tried to second-guess every decision and every movement. As soon as the sun started to come up, Colonel Bartlett heard cannon fire coming from the south down in Harpers

Ferry. It was the sound of the big guns that awakened him from his reverie of yesterday's battle. As the guns roared he paced nervously around his camp. Finishing his coffee he angrily threw the last couple of swallows and the coffee grounds into the fire.

"Where in the hell is that messenger?" growled the Colonel to one of his men. "He left here over an hour ago, damn it."

"Do you want me to go look for him, sir?" asked the soldier.

"No!" barked back Bartlett. "Then I'd have to send someone to go and find you. We're going to need every last man this morning if we're going to stand a chance to keep Harpers Ferry from falling into enemy hands. From the sounds of those guns it may already be too late."

Just then the messenger returned from the Shafer farm.

"Orders from General Slocum, sir," said the soldier as he hurriedly dismounted his horse. "We're to wait for General Franklin, sir. He said that the General was still resting but had given orders to waken him at 7 A.M. sharp, and he'll personally inspect the battle field this morning once he arrives."

"7 A.M. sharp!" Bartlett practically shouted. "Confound that man," he muttered to himself. But orders are orders, thought Bartlett. He's the General. The Colonel gave orders to his men to cook breakfast as the guns less than five miles down the road blasted away. He told them to be quick about it, though. He wanted every man ready to march as soon as General Franklin arrived.

Approximately thirty minutes later, General Franklin, surrounded closely on either side by Generals Slocum and Smith, galloped up the slope of Crampton's Gap and joined Bartlett and his men. General Franklin had a fresh white bandage wrapped around his head and looked a little shaky on his horse.

"Good morning, General Franklin, I trust your head is better this morning. That was a nasty bump you took last night," said Colonel Bartlett.

"Never mind my head, Colonel. I'm fine," grumbled General Franklin. "What can you report to me about the enemy's position?"

"Sir, our scouts report that there's a large force of Confederates with heavy artillery up on Maryland Heights firing down on our troops in Harpers Ferry. They also report that judging from the smoke on the other two ridges, Loudon Heights and School House Ridge, it appears the enemy has the fort in Harpers Ferry surrounded and is barraging the town from all three mountain tops. The cannon fire started up at day break, sir," said the Colonel.

"I know the cannon fire started at day break, Colonel Bartlett! Just because I have a bump on my head doesn't mean my ears stopped working!" yelled General Franklin. "Prepare the men to march, sir."

"Yes, sir!" replied Bartlett. As soon as the words had left Colonel Bartlett's lips, the cannon fire from down the road ceased. Colonel Bartlett and the party of Generals all looked around at each other and then sheepishly looked away.

"Well, what are you waiting for, Bartlett, let's go! Have the men fall in for God's sake, sir." Colonel Bartlett gave the order for the men to march, and they headed south down the Weverton-Rohrersville Road. The silence of the guns that had been roaring so loudly all morning was eerily quiet. The sound of soldiers' footsteps marching on the road now filled the ears of the Union soldiers.

"Those Rebs put up a hell of a fight yesterday to try and hold South Mountain," one of Bartlett's men whispered to the Colonel.

"Yes, they did, indeed," replied Colonel Bartlett. "And our men fought valiantly to take the mountain. But unfortunately we were a half a day late."

EPILOGUE

Rebecca Burgard and Captain Dunning

Riding Rebecca's horse Crescent, Captain Dunning was able to catch up to his regiment, which had retreated a few miles south on the Weverton-Rohrersville Road. The wound in his leg had caused him to lose a lot of blood, though. A makeshift hospital had been made at Saint Luke's Episcopal Church in Brownsville. Daniel Yourtee was there, helping with the wounded when the Captain came riding in and he recognized Rebecca's horse immediately.

"Excuse me, sir, where did you get that horse?" asked Daniel.

"She was wandering on the mountain up near Gapland where we were fighting, and when I got this bullet in the leg, I got some fellows to help me up on her. Would you be so kind to help me down, young man?" replied Captain Dunning.

Daniel helped the Captain down off the horse and into the church where some doctors were busy treating the wounded soldiers. After making sure that Captain Dunning was being looked after, he rode Crescent back to the Burgard farm, put her in her stall in the barn, and gave her a good brushing. Then he fed her some oats and filled up her water bucket.

Captain Dunning's wound was so severe that he was allowed to return home to Georgia to convalesce. Gangrene set in and the leg had to be amputated below the kneecap, so the good soldier had to set out the rest of the war back at home. A year later, Mrs. Dunning died giving birth to their second son. Captain Dunning never forgot the brave young red-headed Rebecca who had helped him on that bloody Sunday in Pleasant Valley. When the war ended he wrote to her, and told her of the loss of his young wife. He asked permission from her father to visit and court her. They were married and Rebecca gave him two more sons and a lovely little daughter with a head of red hair just like Rebecca's.

When Rebecca's parents passed away, the Dunning family continued to farm the old family place at Pleasant Hill.

Tommy Krause and Julia Brown

Tommy Krause and Julia Brown were married almost one year after that bloody Sunday, September 14, 1862. The Brown family gave them a few acres across the road from the Brownsville Store where they built a cabin home. In addition to Tommy's musical prowess as the best fiddler around Pleasant Valley for miles, he was also handy with tools. His best friend, Jeff Higgins, had apprenticed with a local blacksmith. Tommy and Jeff set up a wheelwright's shop, making and repairing wagon wheels, shoeing horses, and doing any general repairs the local farmers and merchants needed. Generations later, when the first automobiles appeared, the Krause's grandsons opened the first garage for mechanical repairs in the same big barn that Tommy and Jeff had built.

Julia gave Tommy a beautiful daughter they named Allison who grew to be the spitting image of her mother. Jeff learned to play the banjo and guitar, and the two friends provided musical accompaniment at local dances around Pleasant Valley for years and years.

Billy, Bessie and Otis "Burgard"

When President Lincoln's Emancipation Proclamation went into effect on January 1, 1863, Rebecca's father, Jacob, offered Billy, Bessie, and Otis their freedom. Billy and Bessie were overwhelmed by this new prospect. They didn't know anyone in Maryland except the Burgards, and the thought of striking it out on their own in a strange country with a war still going on frankly scared the hell out of them. Billy and Bessie sat down at the kitchen table with the Burgards and discussed their's and their son's future. Billy asked Jacob if he and Bessie could go on working for them at Pleasant Hill as a free man and woman. Jacob was happy to oblige them because he truly needed their help. He proposed fair wages to pay them and offered them the small piece of land with some fields and the cabin they were already living in. Jacob had papers drawn up granting them their freedom, so no matter what the outcome of the war they were all free. Under Rebecca's tutelage, Otis continued his studies and in addition to his reading and writing developed quite a head for figures. When Billy and Bessie took their crops to market, Otis always accompanied them and made sure that the family wasn't cheated when the monies were counted out. By the time the war finally ended in 1865, Otis was eighteen years old and had consumed all of the book learning that Rebecca was able to teach him. The Burgard family, all of them, Jacob, and Billy chipped in and sent Otis to the Negro College in Baltimore where he studied business and economics. When Otis graduated, he took a job at the First Negro Bank of Baltimore as a teller. In just four short years, Otis was promoted to the president of the bank. Throughout his forty some years as president of the bank, Otis supported the local negro community in Baltimore and served on many boards and committees advancing the cause of freedom for all Americans.

Daniel Yourtee

The days and weeks to come after the Battle of Crampton's Gap and Antietam held a lasting effect on the sixteen-year-old Daniel Yourtee. The carnage of bodies and wounded soldiers from the two battles, which he and his neighbors had help treat in the hospitals set up in the local churches and homes, weighed heavily on his young mind. Daniel had been raised in the Christian faith and had serious reservations about enlisting in the war even before it came to Pleasant Valley. When it came right down to it, Daniel knew in his heart he couldn't kill another human being. He didn't even like to go hunting for squirrels or rabbits because he couldn't bear for their little bodies to go cold after shooting them.

Daniel had had long and serious discussions with his parents and the minister at his church about war and the commandment -- Thou shalt not kill. His minister told him about an organization formed out of the YMCA in November of 1861 in New York called the United States Christian Commission whose mission was to "promote the spiritual and temporal welfare of the soldiers in the Army and the sailors in the Navy." Local associations of the group had formed in several cities, including Baltimore. Daniel joined the association in Baltimore and became a Delegate. He and others like him in the Christian Commission were often the first responders to show up as soon as the battles were over, delivering water, food and medical supplies to the wounded still strewn about the battlefield. Members of the Christian Commission invented the "soldier's check" that provided a trusted form of currency for Union soldiers to be able to send their earnings back home to their loved ones. Before that, the soldiers were paid in cash in the field. The USCC also came up with the first form of "dog tags," body identifiers, which were small, personalized Bibles that the soldiers could pin to the backs of their uniforms. Initially publishing a collection of familiar hymns, Bible readings, and prayers, the group grew until they had five thousand agents in the field and distributed over ninety-five thousand packages. In the four years of it's existence, the Christian Commission raised and spent over six million dollars in aid to the Union forces (an amount equivalent to almost eighty million dollars in today's monies). After the war ended, Daniel studied at the seminary in Baltimore, eventually becoming a pastor in one of the local churches. Although he often regretted not being able to marry the lovely Julia Brown, his childhood sweetheart, he never failed to visit the Krause's and shower the lovely daughter, Allison, with gifts every time he came home to see his folks at Greystone.

Source: nwuscc.org and the personal collection of USCC pamphlets of Larry McGrain

Major General William Buell Franklin

Not long after the battle at Crampton's Gap, General William Buell Franklin's military career soon became stuck in the mud, sometimes literally. Some locals around Brownsville say that McClellan ordered Franklin and his 6th Corps to march to Antietam on the morning of September 17th via the road through Keedysville. Had Franklin gone that way, he would have arrived on the southern end of the battlefield. Nevertheless, Franklin marched his men up to Boonsboro and then back down the road to Sharpsburg, ending up on the Union's northern flank of the battle. Despite Franklin's protests to be allowed to attack the Confederate left, old General Sumner took over the responsibility of command and refused to allow it, saying that if we failed there, the day would be lost. Some historians have noted that perhaps Franklin's aggressive behavior at Antietam, which was a complete turn around from his actions on September 15th, was because he had been relieved of the responsibility of independent command. Or perhaps he was trying to make up for his failure to rescue the Union garrison at Harpers Ferry.

The dismal failure of the Union forces at the battle of Fredericksburg bode worse for Franklin. The Joint Committee on the Conduct of War (JCCW) placed the majority of blame for the loss directly on William Franklin, and, consequently, the Commander in Chief, Mr. Lincoln lost all confidence in him. He was relieved of his command in the eastern theatre of the war and was eventually sent west to Louisiana to lead troops in the Red River Campaign where he received a not serious, but what proved to be a troublesome, wound in battle. Allowed to return east to convalesce, Franklin was briefly captured by Confederate troops but quickly escaped. While waiting for orders in his hometown of York, Pennsylvania he lent his advice and support to the Union commanders at the Battle of Gettysburg. After Lincoln won re-election over Franklin's friend and former commander George McClellan, Franklin started looking around for a civilian job. His former classmate at West Point, General Ulysses S. Grant, who by now was in command of Lincoln's army, tried repeatedly to convince his boss to give a large command to his friend, William Franklin, but Lincoln would not concede. With the surrender of the Confederacy on April 12, 1865 and Lincoln's assassination two days later, Franklin knew his time in the army was soon to be up. After briefly considering other civilian jobs, in October of 1865, Franklin was offered the position of vice president of manufacturing at Colt Patent Firearms Manufacturing Company in Hartford, Connecticut. For more than twenty years Franklin managed the daily affairs of Colt Firearms, which not only included managing the labor force but also tasks like analyzing steel forged by the new Bessemer process. He oversaw Colt's contract with the Army to produce the new Gatlin guns, which preceded the modern-day machine guns, and utilizing his skills as an engineer, designed and oversaw the construction of Colt's new fire-proof armory building that replaced the one that had burned.

In 1889, shortly after Franklin had retired from Colt, he was asked to serve as the Chief Commissioner to the Paris Exposition, a position that was approved by a joint resolution of Congress. He did a magnificent job, helping the US exhibitors win the lion's share of awards presented and bringing in the whole US effort under budget. For his contributions at the *Exposition Universelle de 1889*, the French awarded him the coveted Legion of Honor.

Throughout William Franklin's post military career at Colt, he served the public on many boards and contributed greatly to various causes. In 1880 he became President of the board for the National Home for Disabled Volunteer Soldiers, a group established by Congress in 1865 to support the growing number of disabled soldiers after the Civil War. For twenty years he was re-elected to that post without a dissenting vote. A public servant until almost the end of his life, Franklin resigned his post with the National Home due to ill health in December, 1899. The Board of Managers accepted his resignation "with extreme regret." Nine days after his eightieth birthday, on March 8th, 1903 William B. Franklin died and on March 12th was laid to rest beside his wife, Anna, in the family cemetery in York, Pennsylvania.

Much of the research for this book and for the small part of the story retold here is from Mark A. Snell's biography of William B. Franklin's, *From First To Last, The Life of Major General William B. Franklin.* Mr. Snell has done an excellent job researching and telling the life story of one of the heroes of the Civil War, and I am extremely grateful for the great work he has accomplished. I highly recommend this book to any student of history of America's Civil War.

Colonel Joseph J. Bartlett

Joseph Jackson Bartlett was practicing law in Elmira, New York, before the Civil War. On October 4th, 1862, less than a month after he led the charge up South Mountain to Crampton's Gap, he was promoted to the rank of Brigadier General where he led a brigade of infantry at the Battle of Fredericksburg. In May of 1863 Bartlett lost more than a third of his fifteen hundred men at the Battle of Salem Creek, yet he was still able to maintain order on the battlefield. When General Robert E. Lee's Army of Northern Virginia surrendered at Appomattox Court House, Bartlett was chosen to receive the stacked arms. Coincidence? That the very same man who was most responsible for carrying the day at Crampton's Gap was chosen to receive the arms on the day the south surrendered? Or was it destiny? Could the thought ever crossed Bartlett's mind that had things gone differently back at Pleasant Valley and Sharpsburg, perhaps Lee could have been defeated then, and the war ended two years earlier? But for a few missed chances and opportunities, could countless lives have been spared? Doubtless historians have noted similar chances and opportunities throughout the Civil War, and for that matter, all wars. In the postwar promotions, Bartlett was given a brevet promotion to the rank of Major General. After the war he continued to serve in the army, helping with the reconstruction in the south. In 1867, shortly after Bartlett had resigned his commission with the army and had returned to his law practice in New York, he was appointed by President Andrew Johnson to United States Ambassador to Norway and Sweden. From March, 1885 to July, 1889, he served as Deputy Commissioner of Pensions. He died in Baltimore in 1893 and is buried at Arlington National Cemetery. For most of his life, he suffered from rheumatism due to exposure in the Civil War. In his honor the Grand Army of the Republic's post in Binghamton, New York, where he was born was named after him.

Brigadier General Paul Jones Semmes

Before the outbreak of the Civil War, Paul Jones Semmes was a banker and a plantation owner. General Semmes' memory of the defeat at Crampton's Gap and the dismal role he consequently had in it may have well been foremost on his mind three days later at Antietam because his brigade fought valiantly indeed. There they played a vital role in General McLaws' counterattack of General Sumners' Union II Corps. In fact Sumner was so shocked by the damage inflicted to his division by McLaws' and Semmes' Rebels that he had refused to let Franklin's VI Corps attack the center of the Confederate line, worried that if the Union lost there, they would lose the day. Old General Sumners may have been correct.

General Semmes brigade was to meet up with General Franklin's division again in Chancellorsville, where they held off the advance of Franklin's entire VI Corps. At the Battle of Gettysburg on July 2, 1863, General Semmes was wounded while leading a charge across the Wheatfield. The wound to his thigh would become mortal because Semmes died eight days later in Martinsburg, West Virginia. Semmes told a reporter shortly before he died that "I consider it a privilege to die for my country." General Robert E. Lee, undoubtedly saddened as Semmes was one of twelve commanders lost at Gettysburg, wrote the following about his death: "he died as he had lived, discharging the highest duty of a patriot with devotion that never faltered and courage that shrank from no danger."

HISTORICAL NOTE

The Federal garrison at Harpers Ferry surrendered at approximately 7:15 A.M. on the morning of Monday, September 15, 1862. The Union force of some fourteen thousand men led by Colonel Dixon S. Miles, not hearing any friendly cannon fire coming from the north or west, assumed correctly that no reinforcements were on their way. In fact the Confederates did not let up the artillery fire raining death down on Harpers Ferry until almost 8:00 A.M. that morning (historical accounts differ on the exact timing of when Confederates stopped firing that morning, with some saying it was as late as 11:00 A.M.). By that time Colonel Miles was mortally wounded.

General Robert E. Lee's Maryland Campaign hadn't gone the way he had hoped. When Lee led his troops through the city of Frederick, Maryland, he had a broadside printed up and distributed throughout the city, welcoming Marylanders to the Confederate cause. He soon realized he had misjudged the western Marylanders' sympathies. It also didn't help that a copy of Lee's Special Orders Number 191 detailing his plans fell into Union hands and quickly made their way back to General McClellan. Then when Lee's forces were defeated at Fox's, Turner's and Crampton's Gaps on South Mountain (the first time his men had been run off the battlefield), Lee was seriously discouraged. So when he received word late on Sunday morning that the Federal garrison at Harpers Ferry had been captured by Stonewall Jackson and General McLaws, his spirits revived. Some historical accounts even suggest that before the seizure of Harpers Ferry, Lee was seriously contemplating retreating his forces back across the Potomac into Virginia.

General William Buell Franklin made a mistake on the evening of Sunday, September 14th when he decided to return to the Shafer farm back in Burkittsville, rather than to make camp at Crampton's Gap for the evening. Had he been able to scout his enemy's position at daybreak (around

5:40 A.M.) on Monday morning, he might have been able to attack Confederate General Lafayette McLaws' rear and thereby perhaps have prevented the early surrender of the Federal garrison at Harpers Ferry. Later in Franklin's own notes he wrote:

As I was crossing the mountain about 7 A.M., on September 15, I had a good view of the enemy's force below, which seemed to be posted on hills stretching across the valley, which is at this place about two miles wide. When I reached General Smith we made an examination of the position, and concluded that it would be suicidal to attack it. The whole breadth of the valley was occupied, and batteries swept the only approaches to the position. We estimated the force as quite as large as ours, and it was in a position which, properly defended, would have required a much greater force than ours to have carried it.

General McClellan had sent orders to General Franklin at approximately 1 A.M. on the morning of

Monday, September 15th to "occupy with your command the road from Rohrersville to Harpers Ferry, placing a sufficient force at Rohrersville" to stymie any possible attack from Confederates retreating from Turner's and Fox's Gaps. General McClellan also repeated what he had told Franklin in his September 13th order: relieve Colonel Miles in Harpers Ferry "by attacking and destroying as much of the enemy as you may find in Pleasant Valley." But it appears General Franklin was satisfied with his victory the day before on Sunday and had no intention to take any chances of being beaten on the battlefield on Monday. Franklin dispatched a brigade and a battery from Couch's division to Rohrersville, but he still had most of Couch's division under his control, and none of these men had been in any of the day's previous battle having come up to Burkittsville too late to join the action. Franklin sent a dispatch to McClellan at 8:50 A.M. describing the situation in Pleasant Valley as it appeared to him: The "enemy is drawn up in line of battle about two miles to our front, one brigade in sight. As soon as I am sure that Rohrersville is occupied, I shall move forward to attack the enemy. This may be two hours from now." As aptly stated in Mark A. Snell's excellent biography of Franklin, *From First to Last, The Life of Major William B. Franklin,* "Franklin already had squandered over three hours of daylight, and yet he predicted that he would not be ready to attack McLaws for two more hours." The fact that Franklin had no intention of attacking is further reinforced by the last line in Franklin's 8:50 A.M. dispatch, "If Harpers Ferry has fallen--and the cessation of firing makes me fear that it has--it is my opinion that I should be strongly reinforced."

Twenty-six years later, General McLaws, responding to a letter Franklin had written to the *Philadelphia Weekly Press* stated that:

General Franklin had ample time on the morning of the 15th to have advanced his forces and engaged mine, which were in line, but a mile and a half distant from Crampton's Gap, and that the sound of his cannon would have been a notice to the garrison in Harper's Ferry that relief was coming, and as his guns would have been fired directly toward Harper's Ferry, which was not three miles distant, in an air-line, they would doubtless have been heard by the garrison.

Students and writers of history have been asking the question, "what if?" since the beginning of time.

What if Confederate Brigadier General Paul Semmes had not been so steadfastly convinced that the Union forces were going to come through Brownsville Pass instead of nearby Crampton's Gap a mile north up South Mountain? Would the Rebels have been able to hold them back entirely on Sunday, September 14th? In that case it may not have mattered anyway that Franklin refused to attack Harpers Ferry at first light on the morning of Monday, September 15th. Harpers Ferry would have fallen anyway.

What if Franklin hadn't foolishly wasted those couple of hours outside Jefferson waiting for Couch's Division to come up and join him? Would he and his Sixth Corps had gotten to Burkittsville early enough to run the Confederates back over South Mountain sooner and come to Colonel Miles and his garrison in Harpers Ferry's rescue?

What if the Federal garrison in Harpers Ferry hadn't fallen? Would Lee have retreated his Army of Northern Virginia back across the Potomac into Virginia to live to fight another day? Could there possibly not even have been a battle of Antietam three days later, the bloodiest battle in America's history, where 22,717 men perished?

The farmhouse that served as Union General William Franklin's headquarters, the Martin Shafer Farm, as it appears in 2017 is located just east of Burkittsville, Maryland. It has been purchased by the Burkittsville Preservation Association and is currently being restored through donations to BPA.

www.burkittsvillepreservationassociation.org

Made in the USA
Lexington, KY
25 November 2019